Table of Contents:

Introduction:

In the depths of our collective human experience, we have faced traumas that have shaken us to our core and battled with addictions that threatened to consume us whole. Yet, within each one of us, there lies an extraordinary strength—a celestial warrior known as the Starseed. It is this very essence that fuels our capacity to rise above adversity, to reclaim our lives, and to inspire others along the path of recovery.

In this transformative journey, we embark upon a quest that transcends the bounds of trauma and addiction. "Many lives of Starseed: Embracing the Starseed Within Us All" is a guiding light, a roadmap that leads us through the labyrinth of our struggles, illuminating the way towards healing, growth, and a brighter future.

Within the pages of this book, you will find the collective wisdom of survivors—individuals who have journeyed through the depths of despair and emerged as beacons of hope. Their stories serve as a testament to the resilience of the human spirit, demonstrating the indomitable power that lies within every one of us.

We delve deep into the intricacies of trauma and addiction, exploring the profound impact they have on our emotions, thoughts, and behaviors. By unraveling the complex web of our struggles, we gain a deeper understanding of ourselves and others, opening the door to empathy, compassion, and forgiveness.

But recovery is not a solitary path. It is within the embrace of a supportive community that we truly find solace and strength. Together, we learn to wield the power of our words, offering encouragement and guidance to those who still walk in the shadows. We discover the transformative force of education and knowledge, empowering ourselves and others with the tools to break free from the chains that bind us.

As we journey through these pages, we encounter practical strategies and insights that breathe life into our recovery. We discover the importance of self-care, the significance of building a strong support system, and the necessity of addressing the underlying issues that fuel our struggles. We learn to set realistic goals, celebrate our victories, and cultivate a mindset of gratitude and forgiveness.

"Many lives of Starseed" is an invitation to embrace our innate Starseed nature, to awaken the warrior within, and to forge a path towards a better life—not only for ourselves, but for all those whose lives we touch. It is a declaration that recovery is not an elusive dream, but a tangible reality waiting to be embraced.

So, let us embark on this transformative journey together. Let us rise from within, overcome the darkness, and illuminate the world with our resilience, compassion, and unwavering spirit. As Starseed, we possess the power to heal, to inspire, and to create a future where the echoes of trauma and addiction are replaced by the harmonious symphony of recovery, growth, and hope.

Meet Star Seed...#1!

The air hung heavy with a sense of foreboding as young Starseed trudged through the poverty-stricken streets of her childhood. Dilapidated buildings loomed overhead, their broken windows like jagged teeth ready to devour any semblance of hope that dared to flicker within her heart. Innocence was a currency that held no value in this desolate place, where vulnerability was exploited, and dreams were crushed beneath the weight of despair.

Starseed's footsteps echoed hollowly as she made her way through the labyrinthine alleys, her eyes darting nervously from side to side. She knew all too well the dangers that lurked in the shadows, waiting to pounce on unsuspecting prey. The streets were a hunting ground for predators who prowled in search of easy targets, their hunger for power and control fueling their insidious deeds.

Her childhood had been marred by a darkness that clung to her like a relentless shadow. It was a world devoid of love and nurturing, where trust was a luxury, she could ill afford. In this treacherous landscape, the very people who were meant to protect her had become the source of her deepest pain.

Her father, a man once filled with dreams and aspirations, had succumbed to the demons that haunted his soul. He drowned his sorrows in the bottom of a bottle, his rage and frustration boiling over into acts of violence that scarred her both physically and emotionally. Starseed bore the bruises and welts as a constant reminder of the love she had never received.

Her mother, worn down by life's hardships, had retreated into a shell of resignation. She turned a blind eye to Starseed's suffering, numbed by her own silent battles. The lines etched on her face told stories of broken dreams and shattered hopes, leaving little room for sympathy or compassion.

Alone and abandoned, Starseed learned to navigate this hostile world with a caution that belied her tender years. She became adept at evading the clutches of danger, her survival instincts sharpened to a razor's edge. She learned to move silently, to blend into the shadows, and to conceal her vulnerability beneath a facade of steely determination.

But beneath the stoic exterior, Starseed's heart ached with a longing for something more. She yearned for the warmth of a loving embrace, for a gentle voice to chase away the demons that haunted her dreams. In the darkest corners of her heart, a flicker of hope dared to burn, refusing to be extinguished by the harsh realities of her existence.

Hold your breath, as Starseed faced her darkest hour. The weight of the world pressed upon her frail shoulders, threatening to crush her spirit. But in that crucible of despair, something stirred within her. A fire ignited, fueled by the remnants of her shattered innocence and the defiant spark of hope.

And so, with trembling hands and a resolute heart, she made her choice. She would not surrender to the darkness that threatened to consume her. She would rise above it, propelled by the flicker of hope that refused to be snuffed out. With every ounce of strength, she could muster, Starseed summoned the courage to confront her demons head-on.

She sought solace and refuge in the power of education. Despite the limitations imposed upon her by her circumstances, Starseed clung to her books like lifelines. In the realm of knowledge, she found an escape from the harsh realities that plagued her existence. Through reading, she explored worlds far beyond the confines of her poverty-stricken neighborhood. She devoured words like a starving soul, hungry for the wisdom and insight they offered.

In the quiet corners of her makeshift sanctuary, Starseed immersed herself in stories of resilience, triumph over adversity, and the boundless potential of the human spirit. She discovered heroes and heroines who faced challenges like her own, and their tales inspired her to believe in the possibility of a better life.

With each turn of the page, Starseed's determination grew. She realized that her circumstances did not define her. She possessed within her the power to rewrite her story, to break free from the chains that bound her to a life of despair. Education became her weapon, her key to unlocking a future filled with promise.

The journey was not without its setbacks. Starseed faced obstacles at every turn. The specter of poverty loomed large, threatening to snatch away her dreams. But she refused to let adversity extinguish her flame. She sought out scholarships, worked multiple jobs, and tirelessly pursued

every opportunity to further her
education.

Slowly, with unwavering perseverance,
Starseed began to carve a path for
herself. She excelled in her studies,
surpassing even her own expectations.
Her resilience and determination caught
the attention of mentors and advocates
who recognized her potential. They
became her guiding lights, offering
support and encouragement when the
weight of the world threatened to
overwhelm her.

Through their guidance, Starseed
discovered her own strength. She
realized that her past did not have to
define her future. The scars she carried

were not marks of shame but symbols of her resilience. In the crucible of her darkest hour, she had forged a spirit that could not be broken.

A Shattered Life #2

Starseed stood at the edge of the chasm, her heart pounding in her chest. The dark abyss before her mirrored the emptiness she felt inside. Her life, once vibrant and full of promise, had been shattered into a thousand pieces.

Just a year ago, she had been a celebrated young artist, her work adorning galleries and captivating the souls of those who beheld it. But it was all a façade. Beneath the surface, a storm raged within her, threatening to consume everything she held dear.

It had started with a tragedy—a devastating fire that claimed the lives of her parents and reduced her childhood home to ashes. The flames had licked at her innocence, leaving scars that ran deeper than the physical. With her family gone, Starseed felt adrift in a world that suddenly seemed alien and hostile.

Seeking solace, she had turned to her art, pouring her anguish onto the canvas. But the pain only grew, festering like an open wound. Her once vibrant colors turned dark and twisted, reflecting the turmoil within her soul. And as her artwork darkened, so did her spirit.

Her descent into darkness reached its nadir on that fateful night, when she found herself standing on the precipice of that chasm. The weight of her grief threatened to pull her into its depths, to swallow her whole. It was in that moment that she made a choice—a choice to fight, to claw her way back from the brink.

renewed determination, Starseed turned her back on the abyss and set out on a journey of redemption. She traveled to far-off lands, seeking wisdom and enlightenment from sages and mystics. She immersed herself in the teachings of ancient philosophies, desperate to find meaning in her shattered existence.

But the path to healing was not an easy one. Starseed faced trials and tribulations that tested her resolve. She encountered treacherous terrain, both physical and emotional, and battled her own inner demons at every turn. Yet, with each obstacle overcome, she felt a glimmer of hope rekindling within her.

As she journeyed, Starseed met fellow travelers who had their own scars, their own stories of resilience. They shared their tales of survival, of rebuilding their lives from the ashes of despair. In their presence, Starseed found solace and strength. She realized that she was not alone in her struggle, that there were others who had faced similar darkness and emerged stronger for it.

newfound resilience, Starseed continued her quest for healing. Along the way, she discovered the power of self-forgiveness, learning to let go of the guilt and self-blame that had haunted her since the fire. She embraced her pain, not as a burden, but as a catalyst for growth and transformation.

And as she delved deeper into her art, Starseed found her colors slowly returning. Her brushstrokes became bolder, more vibrant, mirroring the strength and resilience she had discovered within herself. Her artwork became a testament to her journey, a visual narrative of redemption and healing.

As Starseed ventured further into her journey, she encountered a community of kindred spirits—fellow artists, musicians, and creatives who had found solace in their craft. Together, they formed a sanctuary where they could share their stories, inspire one another, and heal through artistic expression.

In this nurturing environment, Starseed's art flourished. Her canvases became windows into her soul, reflecting not only her pain but also her resilience, hope, and the beauty she had discovered amid darkness. Her work began to resonate with others, touching hearts and igniting conversations about the human experience.

But just as Starseed's spirit began to soar, a new challenge emerged. A rival artist, known for his provocative and controversial pieces, sought to undermine her progress. He taunted her with biting critiques and attempted to overshadow her art with his own shockingly bold creations.

At first, Starseed was shaken by his attacks. Doubt crept back into her heart, threatening to unravel the progress she had made. But instead of retreating into the shadows, she found her voice. With unwavering determination, she confronted her rival, challenging his motives and refusing to let his words define her worth.

The confrontation ignited a spark within Starseed—an unyielding fire to prove herself, not only to her rival but also to herself. She poured her emotions onto the canvas, creating a collection of artworks that defied expectations and pushed the boundaries of her own creativity. Her pieces became a symphony of colors, textures, and emotions—each stroke a testament to her resilience and defiance.

As her art gained recognition, Starseed's journey took on a new purpose. She became an advocate for mental health, using her platform to raise awareness and support for those who had been shattered by their own traumas. Through exhibitions, workshops, and collaborations, she created spaces for healing and encouraged others to find their own paths to redemption.

But amidst the triumphs, Starseed still carried remnants of her past. The scars remained, serving as a reminder of the darkness she had conquered. In a moment of vulnerability, she opened up to a trusted friend, sharing the depths of her pain and the lingering doubts that haunted her. And in that exchange, she discovered the power of genuine connection and the healing that comes from being truly seen and understood.

With her friend's support, Starseed embarked on a new chapter—one of self-acceptance and self-love. She learned to embrace her scars as symbols of strength and resilience. No longer defined by her shattered past, she emerged as a beacon of hope—a testament to the transformative power of healing and the indomitable spirit of the human soul.

A Journey from Darkness to Light

#3

Starseed's footsteps echoed through the desolate alley, each step a heavy reminder of the treacherous path she had chosen. Her heart pounded against her chest, a wild rhythm of fear and anticipation. The flickering streetlights cast long, haunting shadows, painting the world in hues of desperation and despair.

As she ventured deeper into the belly of the city's underbelly, the stench of decay and shattered dreams assaulted her senses. Dimly lit doorways beckoned with false promises, their siren calls luring in lost souls like her own. Starseed had become a mere pawn in this twisted game, where survival meant surrendering her body and soul to the highest bidder.

The world she had once known had crumbled around her. The dreams she had nurtured were replaced by a cold, harsh reality. It was a world where vulnerability was exploited, where dignity became a distant memory. Each night, she donned a mask of false confidence, concealing the fragments of her shattered self beneath layers of makeup and forced smiles.

But amidst the darkness, a tiny flame flickered within her. Starseed clung to the remnants of her dreams, finding solace in one thing—the written word. In the quiet corners of her mind, she weaved stories that transported her to faraway lands. The pen became her sword, and the paper her shield, as she fought against the demons that threatened to consume her.

With each passing day, Starseed discovered the strength to resist the suffocating grip of her circumstances. She sought solace in libraries and coffee shops, immersing herself in the worlds created by others. And slowly, ever so slowly, she began to put her own thoughts to paper, giving voice to the pain and triumphs that echoed within her soul.

Her words became a lifeline, a beacon of hope cutting through the darkness. In the secret corners of her room, Starseed poured her heart onto the pages, crafting a narrative that defied the ugliness that surrounded her. Through her writing, she found a voice that demanded to be heard— a voice that refused to be silenced.

With each stroke of the pen, she wove tales of resilience and redemption. Characters sprang to life, their struggles and triumphs mirroring her own. Through their journeys, she discovered her own strength, her own capacity for growth. The power of her words became a catalyst for change, not only within herself but also in the hearts of those who read her stories.

As the ink stained the paper, it marked a transformation—a journey from darkness to light. Starseed's writing became a vessel for healing, a way to reconcile the pain of

her past and pave the way for a brighter
future. Through her stories, she reached out
to others who had walked similar paths,
offering them solace and inspiration.

And so, as the city slept, Starseed stayed
awake, pen in hand, allowing her words to
flow like rivers of hope. She knew that her
journey was far from over, but armed with
the power of storytelling, she was ready to
face whatever lay ahead. For within the
confines of her stories, she had found her
true self—a beacon of light, guiding others
out of the darkness and into a world where
dreams could once again flourish.

You are taken deep into Starseed's struggle
and the harsh realities of her world.
However, amidst the darkness, her love for

writing becomes a source of strength and a means of transformation. The power of Starseed's words went beyond the ink on the page. It was a catharsis—a release of emotions too heavy to bear alone. Through her writing, she found solace in pouring out her heart, unburdening herself of the pain that had weighed her down for so long.

With every chapter she wrote, Starseed delved deeper into the recesses of her soul, uncovering buried memories and unspoken truths. She bared her vulnerability, exposing her scars and fears to the world. It was a risk, but one she was willing to take, for she understood that true healing could only come through embracing her wounds.

Chapter after chapter, Starseed's story unfolded, painting a vivid tapestry of human resilience and the indomitable spirit that resides within each of us. Her words danced on the page, carrying the reader through a rollercoaster of emotions—grief, anger, hope, and love. She wanted her readers to feel every raw emotion, to know that they were not alone in their struggles.

As her book gained momentum, Starseed's words resonated with people from all walks of life. They reached out to her, sharing their own stories of darkness and longing for a glimmer of light. They found solace in her words, finding the courage to face their own demons and reclaim their narratives.

But even amidst the newfound recognition and connection, Starseed remained grounded. She never forgot the darkness she had emerged from, the battles she had fought to reclaim her voice. Each success was a reminder of the strength that lies dormant within every individual, waiting to be awakened.

With the turn of every page, Starseed's transformation rippled outwards, touching the lives of those who had lost their way. Her writing became a beacon of hope, lighting the path for others to follow. She became an advocate for the voiceless, using her platform to shed light on the injustices and inequalities that pervaded society.

Starseed's journey was not without its setbacks. There were moments of doubt, where the weight of expectations threatened to extinguish her inner flame. But she refused to be silenced. She drew strength from the stories she had written, reminding herself of the lives she had touched and the impact she had made.

Starseed's book became more than just a collection of words. It became a symbol of resilience, a testament to the human spirit's ability to overcome even the darkest of nights. Through her writing, she had transformed her pain into purpose, her despair into hope.

As the final chapters of her book unfolded, Starseed stood at the precipice of a new beginning. The world that once seemed so bleak and unforgiving had begun to change. Her words had sparked a movement, igniting a collective desire for a better future. And in the process, Starseed had found her own salvation.

The journey from darkness to light was never easy, but it was always worth it. And as Starseed closed the final chapter of her book, she knew that her story was just the beginning—a testament to the enduring power of the written word and the capacity for every individual to rise above their circumstances.

Her journey had been long and arduous, but through her words, she had found her voice, her purpose, and her place in the world. And as she looked out into the horizon, she knew that her story would continue to inspire and empower others to embark on their own journey from darkness to light.

Starseed's writing becomes a catalyst for personal growth, healing, and social change. Her story resonates with readers, inspiring them to confront their own challenges and seek their own paths towards transformation.

Through her words, Starseed became a guiding light for those who had lost their way. People from all corners of the world reached out to her, sharing their stories of pain, resilience, and hope. Each message she received reaffirmed her purpose and fueled her determination to make a difference.

Moved by the outpouring of support and connection, Starseed embarked on a new mission. She organized writing workshops in communities plagued by poverty and despair, providing a safe space for individuals to express themselves through storytelling. She witnessed firsthand the transformative power of words as people discovered their own voices and shared their untold truths.

Starseed's book became a rallying cry, an
anthem for those who had been silenced
for far too long. It gained recognition, not
only within literary circles but also in the
broader world. The media hailed her as a
champion of hope and resilience, shining a
light on the injustices that had hidden in the
shadows.

As her influence grew, Starseed used her
platform to advocate for change. She spoke
at conferences, urging society to address
the systemic issues that perpetuated
darkness and inequality. Her words
reverberated through hearts and minds,
planting seeds of compassion, empathy,
and a collective desire for a brighter future.

But amidst the accolades and the progress, Starseed remained grounded in her own journey. She never forgot the struggles she had faced or the battles that others were still fighting. Every day, she continued to write, pouring her emotions onto the page, sharing her vulnerabilities and victories with her readers.

During it all, Starseed's writing became a mirror for her own growth. As she delved into the depths of her soul, exploring the intricacies of her past, she discovered new layers of strength and resilience. Through her words, she found healing and purpose, and she inspired others to embark on their own paths of self-discovery.

The chapters of Starseed's book continued to unfold, intertwining the personal and the universal. She explored themes of forgiveness, redemption, and the beauty that can emerge from the darkest corners of existence. Each sentence was crafted with care, drawing readers deeper into her world, their emotions entwined with hers.

Through her writing, Starseed redefined what it meant to be a survivor. She shattered societal expectations, dismantling the notion that victims must remain forever trapped in their pain. Her story became a testament to the indomitable human spirit, reminding the world that resilience and hope can flourish, even in the harshest of environments.

Starseed's journey continued, a symphony of emotions, experiences, and the power of the written word. With each chapter, she left an indelible mark on the hearts of her readers, igniting a spark within them that could never be extinguished. Her words became a source of solace, inspiration, and a catalyst for change.

In the end, Starseed's book was more than a collection of pages bound together. It was a testament to the transformative power of storytelling and the resilience of the human spirit. It stood as a beacon of hope in a world that often seemed bleak, reminding us of all that our stories have the power to shape our lives and the lives of those around us.

As Starseed closed the final chapter of her book, she knew that her journey had only just begun. With her pen as her sword and her words as her shield, she would continue to navigate the depths of the human experience, uncovering the hidden stories that longed to be heard. For in each story, she discovered a glimmer of light, a reminder that even in the darkest of times, hope could prevail.

Echoes of the Past #4

Starseed stood before an old, weathered mirror, her reflection distorted by the cracks that marred its surface. As she gazed into her own eyes, she couldn't help but feel a sense of disquiet. There were shadows lingering in the depths, echoes of her past that whispered secrets she had yet to uncover.

The accolades and recognition she received for her art brought both validation and a subtle unease. She found herself questioning whether she deserved the praise, haunted by doubts that whispered of her brokenness.

Starseed embarked on a solitary journey, delving into the depths of her own psyche. Memories resurface, each one a puzzle piece that slowly unravels the mysteries of her past. Starseed unearths forgotten moments, fragments of memories that hold the key to understanding the tangled web of her existence.

As Starseed digs deeper, she begins to connect the dots. The true extent of the abuse she endured, the identities of those who betrayed her trust—each revelation shatters the fragile peace she had forged within herself.

But amidst the chaos of these discoveries, Starseed refuses to be consumed by despair. She realizes that her past does not define her, that she has the power to rewrite her own narrative. With newfound clarity, Starseed sets out on a mission to seek justice and closure.

Moments in Hell

The night was heavy with anticipation as Starseed stood before the weathered wooden door. It was the entrance to the house where her nightmares were born, where her innocence was stolen, and where the echoes of her past reverberated through the walls. She took a deep breath, summoning every ounce of courage within her, and pushed open the door.

Inside, the air was stale, carrying the weight of forgotten secrets. The dim light filtering through dusty windows cast long shadows on the worn floorboards. Starseed's footsteps echoed in the silence as she made her way through the abandoned rooms. Each creaking floorboard seemed to whisper a tale of pain and betrayal.

As she explored, memories surged to the surface like an unstoppable tide. She traced her fingertips along the peeling wallpaper, her mind flooded with images of a younger self, seeking solace within these very walls. The laughter and joy she once felt here seemed like distant echoes, overshadowed by the darkness that lurked in every corner.

In the old attic, she stumbled upon a box—a forgotten treasure trove of the past. With trembling hands, she lifted the lid, unleashing a flood of emotions. Photographs spilled out; frozen moments captured in time. She studied each image, her heart aching with the weight of bittersweet nostalgia.

Amidst the faded photographs, she discovered a journal—her own journal from a lifetime ago. Its pages were worn, filled with the heartfelt musings of a young girl yearning for escape. Starseed's fingers traced the words, her eyes devouring the intimate confessions and hidden dreams. The passages painted a vivid portrait of her inner turmoil, laying bare the fragments of a shattered soul.

Lost in the labyrinth of her memories, Starseed found herself reliving pivotal moments. She closed her eyes and was transported to the night she first met him— the one who shattered her trust and innocence. The room came alive around her—the flickering candlelight, the suffocating scent of roses, the sound of his voice coaxing her into a web of deception.

She allowed herself to fully immerse in the memory, feeling the same raw vulnerability that consumed her on that fateful night. As the memories continued to unravel, Starseed unearthed letters—forgotten fragments of communication that shed light on the tangled web of her past. Each letter revealed another layer of deception, another person complicit in her suffering.

With determination burning in her eyes, Starseed vowed to confront those who had shattered her world. Each encounter But as Starseed delves deeper into her investigation, she realizes that the truth she seeks is elusive. As the night is ending, Starseed discovers a faded photograph tucked away in a forgotten corner of the house. It reveals a face she never expected to see—the missing link that could unravel the web of secrets and lead her closer to the truth.

The photograph is a fragment of a puzzle, a tantalizing glimpse into a hidden world. Starseed's heart races with anticipation as she embarks on a quest to uncover the identity of the person in the photograph, knowing that it holds the key to unlocking the secrets of her shattered past.

Driven by an insatiable curiosity, Starseed sets off on a relentless pursuit of information. She scours old archives, tracks down long-lost acquaintances, and delves into the darkest corners of her memories.

Starseed uncovers shocking revelations that challenge her understanding of the world she thought she knew. Betrayals, long buried beneath layers of deceit, are exposed, leaving her breathless and filled with a mixture of anger, sorrow, and determination. As she pieces together the fragments of her shattered life, Starseed grapples with a myriad of emotions—grief, anger, forgiveness, and a fierce determination to reclaim her sense of self.

A Glimmer Of HOPE! #5

Starseed's journey began with a shimmering hope in her eyes and a fire burning within her soul. From a young age, she had always felt different, restless in the confines of the ordinary. Her dreams stretched across galaxies, and her aspirations knew no bounds. She craved adventure, seeking to carve her own path in a world that often felt too small for her vibrant spirit.

Born into a humble family, Starseed grew up in a small town where dreams were whispered but rarely pursued. But she was determined to break free from the shackles of convention and embrace the vast expanse of possibilities that awaited her. With an unyielding optimism, she set out on a quest to discover her true self and make her mark on the world.

As she embarked on her journey, Starseed encountered many trials and tribulations. She faced setbacks and disappointments, but her spirit remained unbroken. She knew that the road to greatness was seldom smooth, and she was willing to endure the challenges that came her way.

However, amidst the backdrop of her soaring dreams, darkness lurked, waiting to ensnare her. Starseed unknowingly crossed paths with an abuser—a wolf in sheep's clothing. At first, his charm masked his true nature, and she fell into his web of manipulation and control.

The journey that was once filled with boundless optimism and dreams now became a twisted maze of pain and confusion. The abuser's hold tightened around her, suffocating her vibrant spirit. He isolated her from friends and family, cutting her off from the support she so desperately needed.

But Starseed was not one to be defeated easily. Deep within her, a flicker of resilience remained. She refused to let the darkness consume her entirely. With each passing day, she fought to reclaim her sense of self, to break free from the shackles that bound her.

Her journey became a battle—a battle for her freedom, her dreams, and her very soul. She found strength in the scars that marked her, each one a testament to her will to survive. With every setback, she rose again, fueled by the fire that burned within her.

As she fought to escape the clutches of her abuser, Starseed discovered a newfound purpose. She realized that her story could serve as a beacon of hope for others who found themselves trapped in similar situations. She resolved to share her experiences, to shed light on the painful reality of abuse, and to offer solace to those who felt lost in the shadows.

With vigor and determination, Starseed reclaimed her voice. She poured her heart and soul onto the pages of her journal, weaving her story with raw emotion and unwavering honesty. Her words became a lifeline for those who had lost their way, a guiding light in the darkest of nights.

"Lost in the Shadows" emerged as a testament to Starseed's resilience and unwavering spirit. It became a powerful memoir, a tale of survival and triumph. Her words resonated with countless others, giving them the courage to break free, to reclaim their lives, and to dream once again.

In the end, Starseed emerged from the darkness, her spirit shining brighter than ever before. She had fought against all odds, defying the chains that sought to bind her. And as she stood tall, she knew that her journey had not been in vain.

Starseed had become a beacon of hope—a testament to the indomitable strength of the human spirit. Her story inspired others to find their own voices, to stand up against abuse, and to never lose sight of their dreams.

With her newfound purpose, Starseed embarked on a mission to raise awareness about abuse and support survivors. She became an advocate, speaking at conferences, sharing her experiences, and offering guidance to those in need. She joined forces with organizations dedicated to combating domestic violence, lending her voice and her story to their cause.

Starseed's journey also led her to connect with fellow survivors, forming a tight-knit community of support and healing. Together, they created a safe space where they could share their stories, find solace in one another's experiences, and rebuild their lives. Through their collective strength, they shattered the cycle of abuse and embraced a future filled with hope and resilience.

In addition to her advocacy work, Starseed found solace in her creative pursuits. She channeled her pain and triumph into art, painting vivid canvases that captured the essence of her journey. Her artwork became a visual representation of the human spirit's ability to rise from the depths of despair and find redemption.

As her story gained recognition, Starseed was approached by publishers who recognized the power of her words. She embraced the opportunity to amplify her message further, and "Lost in the Shadows" transformed into a published memoir, reaching a wider audience hungry for stories of resilience and hope.

The book became a bestseller, resonating with readers around the world. Starseed's story touched hearts, encouraging others to confront their own shadows and find the strength to overcome adversity. She received countless letters and messages from individuals who found solace and inspiration within the pages of her memoir.

But Starseed's journey didn't end with the success of her book. She continued to advocate for change, tirelessly working to raise awareness, educate communities, and support survivors. Her voice rang out, unwavering and resolute, as she fought for a world free from abuse—a world where dreams could flourish without fear.

Years passed, and Starseed's impact continued to grow. She became a symbol of resilience and empowerment, a living testament to the transformative power of the human spirit. Her story became a part of the collective consciousness, inspiring generations to come.

As she reflected on her journey, Starseed felt a deep sense of fulfillment. She had overcome immense adversity and emerged as a beacon of hope. Her dreams, once confined to the realm of imagination, had blossomed into a reality more vibrant and profound than she could have ever imagined.

And so, Starseed's journey, though fraught with pain and darkness, ultimately became a testament to the strength and resilience that lie within each of us. Her story reminded the world that even in the face of the most insurmountable odds, hope can thrive, dreams can be realized, and the human spirit can shine brightly, illuminating even the darkest corners of our existence.

<u>Self-Medication #6</u>

Star Seed was a mere whisper of her former self. Her once vibrant spirit had been eclipsed by the suffocating weight of depression. Each day felt like a relentless storm, tearing at the fabric of her soul. Loneliness clung to her like a second skin, isolating her from the world.

In the depths of her despair, Star found solace in a secret refuge – a dimly lit room adorned with crimson walls, where shadows danced to a haunting melody. This chamber held her salvation, her means to escape the anguish that consumed her.

The scent of incense filled the air, mingling with the heady aroma of marijuana. Star's trembling fingers caressed the rolled joint, her lifeline to temporary bliss. As the smoke curled around her, wisps of reality drifted away, replaced by a surreal dreamscape where her pain faded into obscurity.

With each inhale, she embarked on a journey to a realm where her heartache was hushed, and her worries dissolved like smoke in the wind. The intoxicating haze whisked her away, granting her respite from the haunting memories that tormented her waking hours.

But as the high waned, the storm of emotions would return, fiercer than before. The self-medication had become a double-edged sword, temporarily numbing her anguish while intensifying its grip on her fragile psyche. The escape she sought was transient, leaving her yearning for more.

Her downward spiral continued unabated until one fateful day when she stumbled upon a support group for those battling mental health demons. Reluctantly, she entered the room, her heart pounding in her chest like a trapped bird.

Within those walls, she discovered a mosaic of broken souls, each with their own tale of struggle and redemption. They shared their darkest fears and deepest sorrows, offering support and understanding without judgment. In their presence, Star felt a flicker of hope reignite within her.

Through therapy and the unwavering support of newfound friends, Star began to untangle the knots of her despair. She learned healthier ways to cope with her pain, to confront her demons head-on instead of numbing them with substances.

As time passed, Star's journey of healing unfolded. She shed the shackles of addiction, embracing self-care and self-compassion instead. The room that once held her captive became a relic of the past, a reminder of the darkness she had traversed.

Now, as Star stands on the precipice of her newfound strength, she reaches out to others grappling with similar battles. Her words carry the weight of authenticity, resonating with those who have yet to find their voice. She offers them a glimmer of light, assuring them that even in the darkest of nights, there is hope for a brighter tomorrow.

Star Seed's story is a testament to the power of resilience, the capacity for transformation that lies within each shattered soul. Through her journey, she reminds us that the path to healing may be arduous, but the destination is worth every painful step.

Relapse

In the wake of her newfound strength, a cruel twist of fate threatened to unravel Star Seed's progress. A series of unexpected events sent her spiraling back into the abyss of despair, triggering a relapse that shattered the fragile fragments of her recovery.

The weight of her emotions bore down on her like an avalanche, suffocating any flicker of hope that remained. Desperation gnawed at her core, compelling her to seek solace in the familiar haze she had once escaped to.

With trembling hands, Star reached for the joint that had become her crutch. The room that had once been a relic transformed once again into her sanctuary, its crimson walls closing in around her like a comforting embrace. The familiar scent of incense mingled with the acrid smoke as she inhaled deeply, hoping to drown out the cacophony of pain that threatened to consume her.

For a moment, the smoke enveloped her senses, granting respite from the torment that plagued her mind. But as the intoxication settled, so too did the realization of her relapse. She was trapped in a vicious cycle, desperately seeking escape only to find herself trapped in a labyrinth of addiction.

The guilt and shame crashed over her like a tidal wave, intensifying her emotional anguish. Each failed attempt at breaking free further eroded her self-esteem, leaving her feeling trapped in a never-ending cycle of self-destruction.

Yet, amidst the darkness, a flicker of determination remained. Star knew deep down that she couldn't let her relapse define her. She had tasted moments of clarity and hope, and she clung to them like a lifeline. It was time to summon the strength to rise above her addiction once more.

With renewed resolve, Star sought help once again. She returned to the support group she had abandoned, her heart heavy with remorse but fueled by a glimmer of hope. She faced the consequences of her relapse head-on, admitting her struggles and seeking guidance from those who had walked a similar path.

Through the unwavering support of her newfound friends, Star began to rebuild her shattered foundation. She embraced the lessons learned from her relapse, recognizing the triggers and pitfalls that had led her astray. She sought therapy, delving deeper into the roots of her pain, and developing healthier coping mechanisms to navigate the turbulent storms of her mind.

The road to recovery was far from linear. There were setbacks and moments of doubt, but Star refused to let them define her journey. Armed with the knowledge that relapses were a natural part of recovery, she forged ahead, determined to break free from the chains that bound her.

As time passed, Star's resilience and perseverance prevailed. She emerged from the depths of her relapse with a newfound strength and a deeper understanding of her own vulnerabilities. Her story became a beacon of hope for those who had faltered and lost their way, a testament to the power of resilience and the unyielding spirit of the human heart.

Star Seed's journey was not without its scars, but it was through those scars that she found her true strength. And as she shared her story once more, she ignited sparks of hope in the hearts of others, assuring them that even in the face of relapse, recovery was still possible.

As Star Seed stood before the recovery group and survivor group, a sense of purpose radiated from her. She had come a long way since the depths of her despair, and her voice carried the weight of experience as she narrated her life's journey.

Her words were a tapestry woven with vulnerability, resilience, and hard-won wisdom. She spoke of the crippling grip of depression that had once held her captive, of the allure of self-medication that promised escape but only deepened her pain. She shared the raw details of her relapse, unafraid to expose the cracks in her armor.

But amidst the darkness, Star's narrative shone with flickers of hope. She recounted the pivotal moments of seeking help, the support she found within these very walls. The friendships forged and the therapy sessions that unraveled the tangled knots of her mind.

She described the arduous process of rebuilding her life, piece by fragile peace. The pursuit of healthier coping mechanisms, the dedication to self-care, and the unwavering commitment to her own well-being. She spoke of the setbacks and the triumphs, the moments of doubt and the sparks of resilience that kept her moving forward.

With each word, Star's voice grew stronger, her presence commanding the attention of every listener. She didn't shy away from the realities of recovery, the ongoing battle against relapse or the scars that marked her journey. Instead, she embraced them as symbols of her strength, proof that a life once devastated by depression could be rebuilt, piece by piece.

Her story served as a lifeline for those in the room - a lifeline that whispered, "You're not alone." She spoke directly to the hearts of those who had stumbled and fallen, reminding them that relapse was not the end of their journey but rather another opportunity for growth and renewal.

As Star Seed concluded her narrative, her eyes scanned the room, taking in the faces of those who had listened intently. She saw the flicker of hope in their eyes, the glimmer of possibility that had been rekindled within them.

With a compassionate smile, she extended her hand, offering support, understanding, and a reminder that recovery was a continuous process. She assured them that the road ahead might be challenging, but they were not alone. Through the power of shared experiences, they could navigate the storms and find solace in the unity of their struggles.

And so, Starseed stood tall, a beacon of light amidst the darkness, reminding others that their stories, too, held the power to inspire and heal. With unwavering courage, she vowed to continue sharing her journey, to uplift those who still grappled with their own battles, and to offer a glimmer of hope to those in need.

For in her narrative, Star Seed had discovered her purpose – to be a guiding light, a reminder that even in the depths of despair, there was always a path to recovery, to hope, and to a life filled with renewed joy and meaning.

Street Walker #7

In a world ravaged by a drug-induced haze, amidst the swirling chaos of neon lights and desperate souls, there lived a girl named Starseed. She was a product of her environment, a survivor in a city that thrived on the highs and lows of addiction. Starseed had a past, a history of emotional distress that haunted her every waking moment. And so, she sought solace in the arms of drugs, using them to escape the pain that consumed her.

Starseed's journey began innocently enough, a timid step into a world she had only heard whispers of. She was drawn to a substance known as Bliss, a pill that promised euphoria beyond imagination. With each swallow, the weight of her troubles lifted, and a veil of serenity enveloped her troubled mind. The drug became her gateway, a one-way ticket to a world where pain was muted, and joy knew no bounds.

As Starseed delved deeper into the drug-crazed world, the line between reality and fantasy blurred. Days merged into nights, and she danced through a kaleidoscope of colors and sensations. The city's pulse beat in sync with her own as she navigated through dimly lit alleyways and seedy clubs, searching for her next fix. She became a wanderer, lost in a labyrinth of her own making.

But with each hit, Starseed's descent grew steeper. The initial allure of Bliss faded, leaving her craving more. The once vibrant colors of her existence turned into a muted palette, and her own reflection became a distant memory. She became a ghost, haunting the fringes of society, a mere shell of the person she once was.

As the addiction tightened its grip, Starseed's choices grew reckless. She bartered her body and soul for the next high, trading fragments of her humanity for fleeting moments of ecstasy. The world around her crumbled, consumed by the same drug-fueled madness that plagued her existence. Desperation and despair were the currency of the realm, and Starseed paid her dues with every breath.

In her darkest moments, as the weight of her choices threatened to suffocate her, a flicker of light emerged. It was a glimmer of hope, a reminder that redemption was still within reach. Starseed met a fellow wanderer, a soul as broken as her own, who spoke of a legendary drug known as Redemption. It was whispered to possess the power to heal wounds and restore shattered lives.

With newfound purpose, Starseed embarked on a quest for Redemption. She scoured the city's underbelly, following cryptic clues and risking her life at every turn. The journey was treacherous, but she pressed on, driven by a desperate desire to break free from the chains that bound her.

Finally, after countless trials and tribulations, Starseed found herself standing before a dilapidated building, the rumored birthplace of Redemption. With trembling hands, she pushed open the heavy doors and stepped into a world untainted by addiction. The air was thick with anticipation as she approached a figure cloaked in shadows.

"You seek Redemption," the figure whispered, their voice a wisp on the wind. "But remember, true redemption lies within."

Starseed's heart pounded in her chest as she reached out for the offered vial. With a mix of fear and hope, she swallowed the contents, feeling a surge of warmth spread through her veins. The world around her shifted, and she found herself bathed in a soft, ethereal light. It was as if a veil had been lifted, revealing a clarity she hadn't experienced in years.

As Starseed stood during this transformative moment, memories flooded back to her. She saw fragments of her past, the pain and trauma that had led her down this treacherous path. But this time, she viewed them through a lens of understanding and forgiveness. The weight of her emotional distress began to loosen its grip, replaced by a newfound sense of self-compassion.

With each passing moment, Starseed felt a reawakening of her spirit. She saw the world with fresh eyes, appreciating the beauty and wonder that had been obscured by her addiction. The drug-crazed world she had once known now seemed hollow and shallow, a facade that offered nothing but false promises.

In the days that followed, Starseed embarked on a journey of healing and self-discovery. She sought out support from kindred spirits who had also found solace in the arms of Redemption. Together, they formed a community, a sanctuary where broken souls could find refuge and understanding. Through therapy, art, and connection, they rebuilt their lives, piece by fragmented piece.

Starseed's story became a beacon of hope for those lost in the throes of addiction. Her transformation inspired others to seek their own path to redemption, to confront their emotional distress head-on rather than succumbing to the allure of drugs. She became a symbol of resilience, a testament to the human spirit's capacity to heal and grow.

But Starseed's journey was far from over. As she continued to navigate the complexities of recovery, she realized that the battle against emotional distress was ongoing. The allure of Bliss and the temptations of the drug-crazed world still lingered, like shadows in the corners of her mind. Yet armed with the tools of self-awareness and a newfound strength, she faced each day with unwavering determination.

Starseed's story serves as a reminder that the pursuit of healing is not a linear path. It is a dance of light and darkness, of triumphs and setbacks. It is a journey that requires courage and vulnerability, but one that holds the promise of a life reclaimed.

And so, as we leave Starseed for now, standing at the crossroads of her own destiny, we can't help but crave more. We yearn to witness her continued growth, to see the world through her transformed eyes. For her story is not just one of addiction and despair, but one of resilience, redemption, and the enduring power of the human spirit.

I stand before you today, a testament to the resilience that resides within each one of us. My name is Starseed, and I am on a journey of healing and recovery, just like all of you. Together, we have embarked on a path that demands courage, vulnerability, and an unwavering commitment to our own well-being.

When I look out at this room, I see strength. I see individuals who have faced their own emotional distress head-on, who have confronted the darkness within and refused to let it define them. We have all experienced the allure of drugs and the depths of addiction, each of us ensnared in a world that promised escape but delivered only pain.

But here we are, united in our quest for redemption. We have chosen to step out of the shadows and into the light, reclaiming our lives from the clutches of addiction. Our stories may be different, but they are woven together by a common thread - the desire to heal, to rise above our past, and to create a future filled with hope and purpose.

As we gather in this sacred space, let us remember that recovery is not a destination; it is a lifelong journey. It is a commitment we make to ourselves, to prioritize our well-being and nurture our spirits. It is a choice to face our emotional distress with compassion, to acknowledge the wounds that have shaped us, and to find healthier ways to cope.

In this room, we find strength in one another. We are not alone in our struggles, and we need not carry the weight of our burdens in isolation. Together, we can share our stories, our triumphs, and our setbacks. We can lean on each other for support, encouragement, and understanding.

Let us embrace the power of community, for it is within these walls that we find solace and connection. We are not defined by our past mistakes or the scars we carry. We are defined by the resilience and courage we display in the face of adversity. We are survivors, warriors, and beacons of hope for those who may still be lost in the darkness.

Today, as we gather, let us celebrate the progress we have made on our individual journeys. Let us honor the battles we have fought and the victories we have achieved. But let us also be mindful of the work that lies ahead. Recovery demands our unwavering commitment, our willingness to confront our emotional distress and continue the arduous process of healing.

Together, we have the power to create a ripple effect of transformation. As we reclaim our lives, we inspire others to do the same. Our stories can serve as beacons of hope, guiding those who are still lost toward the path of redemption and recovery.

So, my fellow survivors and warriors, let us stand tall, knowing that we are not defined by our past but rather by the strength and resilience we embody. Let us continue to support one another, to lift each other up when the weight of our emotional distress threatens to overwhelm us.

May we find solace in this community, and may we continue to carve out a future filled with healing, growth, and the boundless possibilities that await us. For we are survivors, and together, we will navigate this journey of recovery, one step at a time.

<u>Willow Brook #8</u>

Once upon a time, in the quaint and picturesque town of Willow brook, nestled amidst rolling green hills and shimmering lakes, there lived a young woman named Star Seed. Her name, an ethereal reflection of her gentle demeanor and vibrant spirit, held a tale of its own. Star Seed was destined to become a living embodiment of the statistics, where the odds were indeed stacked against her.

In this idyllic town, where the simplest of joys were found in the rustle of leaves and the sweet fragrance of wildflowers, darkness lurked beneath the surface. Hidden behind the white picket fences and cozy cottages, a silent battle waged against the insidious force of addiction.

Star Seed's journey began with the whispers of her ancestry, a lineage adorned with the scars of addiction. Embedded within her very DNA lay the genetic predisposition that heightened her vulnerability to the siren call of substances. It was as if the odds had conspired against her, weaving a tapestry of trials and tribulations that would test her resilience.

The townsfolk, blissfully unaware of the ticking time bomb that lay within their midst, reveled in their own innocence. But Star Seed, with her piercing emerald eyes and cascading chestnut locks, bore the weight of her lineage upon her fragile shoulders. She carried the legacy of her forebearers, whose lives had been consumed by the clutches of addiction.

As the seasons danced across the landscape, Star Seed found solace in the beauty that surrounded her. She would wander through meadows, her fingertips grazing the velvety petals of wild roses, absorbing the vibrant colors and delicate fragrances with an almost desperate hunger. The natural world became her sanctuary, a respite from the tumultuous storm that brewed within her soul.

But the whispers grew louder, and the allure of the unknown tightened its grip. Star Seed's path began to intertwine with a group of friends, each fighting their own battles against the darkness that threatened to engulf them. Together, they formed a fragile alliance, seeking solace and understanding in the face of adversity.

The town's landscape, once painted with shades of innocence, now revealed the cracks and crevices of a hidden underbelly. Abandoned buildings, their timeworn walls bearing witness to countless broken dreams, became the backdrop for clandestine meetings and desperate attempts to escape the clutches of addiction.

Starseed, her heart aching with an indescribable longing, found herself tiptoeing along a precipice, teetering between the abyss of addiction and the flickering light of hope. She was acutely aware of the odds stacked against her, the weight of her genetic predisposition threatening to consume her very being.

But within the depths of her soul, Star Seed possessed an unyielding strength. She refused to succumb to the predetermined destiny that awaited her. With steely determination and unwavering resolve, she sought the support of the town's resources, embracing the healing power of therapy, community, and love.

Slowly, but surely, Star Seed's story began to shift. The odds, once firmly stacked against her Slowly, but surely, Star Seed's story began to shift. The odds, once firmly stacked against her, trembled under the weight of her resilience. With every sunrise that painted the sky in hues of gold and rose, she fought to reclaim her life from the clutches of addiction.

The townsfolk, initially oblivious to the struggles that unfolded within their midst, witnessed Star Seed's transformation. They marveled at her unwavering spirit, her unwavering commitment to rewrite her own narrative. Like a phoenix rising from the ashes, she defied the statistics that had threatened to consume her.

Word of Star Seed's triumph spread through the town like wildfire. Her story became a beacon of hope, illuminating the path for others who had lost their way. As the days turned into weeks and weeks into months, the town began to rally around her, offering support, encouragement, and a shoulder to lean on.

The abandoned buildings, once symbols of despair, were reclaimed as spaces of healing and renewal. Community centers and support groups sprouted like wildflowers, offering sanctuary to those seeking solace and strength. Together, Star Seed and her newfound companions forged a bond, united in their shared journey of recovery.

With tenacity as her armor and the support of her community as her shield, Star Seed confronted her demons head-on. She delved into the depths of her soul, sifting through the fragments of her past and piecing them together with newfound wisdom. She discovered the power of self-love, forgiveness, and acceptance as she rebuilt the foundation of her life.

The seasons continued their eternal dance, bearing witness to Star Seed's metamorphosis. With each passing day, she grew stronger, her inner light shining ever brighter. She became a guiding star for others navigating their own treacherous paths, her story a testament to the indomitable human spirit.

As the years unfolded, Willow brook transformed from a town plagued by addiction to a haven of hope and renewal. The statistics that once loomed over Star Seed and her fellow townsfolk lost their power, overshadowed by the collective strength and resilience they had discovered within themselves.

And so, the story of Star Seed, the young woman whose name held the weight of the odds stacked against her, became a living testament to the triumph of the human spirit. Her journey, painted with captivating verbiage and woven with threads of resilience, left an indelible mark on the hearts and minds of all who bore witness.

In the heart of Willow brook, where wildflowers bloomed and the echoes of struggle had been replaced by the melodies of healing, Star Seed's legacy lived on. Her name, once a symbol of statistical predisposition, became a beacon of hope, reminding all who heard it that the human spirit can transcend the limitations imposed upon it.

And so, the story of Star Seed, the young woman who defied the odds and illuminated the path for others, remains etched in the annals of Willow brook's history. Her tale, a masterpiece painted with the brushstrokes of resilience and hope, forever captivates the hearts of those who dare to dream of a brighter tomorrow.

I am humbled and honored to share my story with every one of you. In this sacred space of healing and transformation, I see the strength and resilience that emanates from your souls. You are warriors, victors in your own battles against addiction, and it is with utmost admiration and respect that I recognize your courage in standing here today.

To each survivor who has walked the path of recovery, I salute you. Your journey, though unique and deeply personal, is a testament to the indomitable human spirit. You have faced the darkest corners of your existence, confronted the demons that once held you captive, and emerged as beacons of hope for those who still wander in the shadows.

I acknowledge the sleepless nights, the tears shed in solitude, and the relentless inner battles that have forged you into the resilient souls that you are. You have faced your own statistical predispositions, the odds that seemed insurmountable, and you have defied them with unwavering determination. Your stories, like brushstrokes in a grand tapestry, weave a narrative of triumph over adversity.

Together, we have transformed this once-quiet town of Willow brook into a sanctuary of healing and renewal. Our collective strength and support have breathed life into abandoned buildings, filling them with the warmth of community and the promise of a brighter future. The very ground we stand upon vibrates with the echoes of our shared victories and the whispers of hope for those who are yet to find their way.

In sharing my story, I hope to amplify the voices of all survivors, past.
and present. Each one of you has a tale that deserves to be heard, a story of resilience and redemption that can ignite a flame of inspiration within others. We are not alone, my dear friends, but rather a community of survivors, united by our battles and our triumphs.

Today, I stand here not as a solitary star, but as a constellation of survivors, shining together in a night sky that knows no limits. I am grateful for every single one of you, for the strength and resilience you bring to this circle. It is your unwavering commitment to share your stories, to lend a hand to those in need, that fuels the fire of hope within me.

As I look into your eyes, I see the spark of resilience, the light that refused to be extinguished. I see warriors who have turned their pain into purpose, their struggles into strength, and their stories into beacons of hope for generations to come. Today, I honor each one of you for the battles you have fought and the victories you have achieved.

Let us continue to walk this path together, supporting one another, and extending our hands to those who are still lost in the labyrinth of addiction. Our stories, like drops of water, have the power to create ripples that can transform lives, heal wounds, and ignite the flame of hope in even the darkest corners.

I am eternally grateful to share this space with you, my fellow survivors. May our stories continue to empower others, reminding them that within every statistical predisposition lies the potential for resilience, redemption, and the limitless power of the human spirit.

Thank you, and may our collective light shine bright, guiding others out of the shadows and into the embrace of a new dawn.

<u>Childhood of Pain #9</u>

Starseed's childhood was shrouded in darkness, a tapestry woven with threads of pain and despair. Born into a world where drug use was prevalent, she was destined to navigate treacherous waters from the very beginning.

Her parents, lost in the grip of addiction themselves, were unable to provide the love and care that a child needed. Their lives were consumed by the pursuit of their next high, leaving Starseed to navigate the chaos alone. Unstable family dynamics dictated her existence, and she became a mere spectator in the theater of her own life.

Poverty, like a relentless specter, haunted their dilapidated home. Hunger gnawed at her young bones, an unyielding reminder of their destitution.

Starseed's dreams, once vibrant and full of hope, withered like fragile petals on a forgotten flower. The world beyond her doorstep seemed like an unattainable fantasy, a distant land where happiness and abundance thrived.

But it was the exposure to violence that inflicted the deepest wounds upon her fragile soul. The air in their home was heavy with tension, a volatile storm waiting to unleash its fury. The innocent laughter of childhood was stifled by the chilling echoes of abuse. The bruises that adorned her body were not mere physical marks but symbols of a spirit slowly breaking.

In the darkest corners of her existence, where hope struggled to find a foothold, Starseed sought solace in the only escape she could find. Drugs became her refuge, a temporary respite from the pain that enveloped her like a suffocating fog. The taste of oblivion, the numbing embrace of substances coursing through her veins, offered a fleeting moment of release from the chains that bound her.

The drugs became her companion, her confidant in the lonely hours of the night. With each hit, she danced on the precipice of euphoria and despair, teetering on the edge of a precipice that threatened to consume her. The world outside faded into insignificance, and the void within her grew deeper with every passing day.

Yet, in the depths of her despair, a small flame flickered within Starseed's heart. A spark of resilience, buried beneath layers of sorrow, refused to be extinguished. She yearned for a life beyond the confines of her circumstances, a life where dreams could be realized, and wounds could heal.

In the depths of Starseed's struggle, a chance encounter would ignite a spark of hope within her broken spirit. A kind-hearted stranger, a beacon of compassion amidst the chaos, crossed her path one fateful day. Their eyes met, and in that moment, Starseed felt seen, truly seen, for the first time in her life.

This stranger, a mentor of sorts, recognized the flicker of potential hidden beneath Starseed's hardened exterior. They offered her a lifeline, guiding her towards a path of healing and transformation. With their unwavering support, Starseed began to believe in the possibility of a different future, one where she could break free from the chains of addiction and despair.

Together, they embarked on a journey of self-discovery, delving deep into the crevices of Starseed's past. Through therapy and counseling, the wounds inflicted upon her by her parents' abuse began to heal, layer by layer. The process was painful, unearthing buried memories and emotions that had long been suppressed, but Starseed was determined to find her way back to herself.

As Starseed's inner strength grew, she found solace in alternative healing practices. Meditation and mindfulness became her allies, guiding her towards self-acceptance and inner peace. Nature became her sanctuary, and she sought refuge in its soothing embrace, finding solace in the whispers of the wind and the gentle caress of sunlight.

With time, Starseed's relationship with drugs transformed. No longer a crutch to numb the pain, they became a reminder of the darkness she had emerged from. Through sheer willpower and the support of her newfound community, she learned to resist the allure of substances, embracing healthier coping mechanisms instead.

The road to recovery was far from easy. There were setbacks and moments of doubt that threatened to pull Starseed back into the abyss. But she refused to surrender to her past, determined to create a future that defied the odds. Her resilience and unwavering spirit captivated those around her, inspiring hope in even the most hardened hearts.

As Starseed stood before the survivor group, her voice trembled with a mix of nerves and determination. She was just a teenager, lost in a sea of uncertainty, brought here as a guest to share her story. The weight of her past clung to her like a heavy cloak, but she knew, deep down, that it was important to take this step towards getting clean. Still, she couldn't help but feel overwhelmed by the daunting journey that lay ahead.

"Um, hi everyone," Starseed began, her voice soft yet filled with raw honesty. "I guess you could say I'm new here. I've seen addiction tear apart lives and I've felt its grip on my own. But honestly, I'm not sure how to get from where I am to where I want to be."

A murmur of understanding and empathy rippled through the room. Starseed took a deep breath, drawing strength from the collective presence of those who had walked a similar path.

"I've tried to break free from the chains of addiction before, but it feels like a maze with no clear exit. I want to believe that recovery is possible, that there's light at the end of this dark tunnel. But the truth is, I don't know how to get there," she confessed, her voice a delicate thread of vulnerability.

The room fell silent, the air heavy with shared experiences and unspoken wisdom. Starseed's words hung in the air, waiting for a response, a guiding light to lead her towards the answers she sought.

Then, a voice, weathered by years of struggle, spoke up. "Starseed, we've all been where you are, feeling lost and overwhelmed. Recovery is a journey, and it starts with taking that first step. It's about finding the right support system, whether it's therapy, counseling, or joining groups like this one. It's about surrounding yourself with people who understand and who can help you navigate the challenges ahead."

Another voice chimed in, gentle yet firm. "Starseed, it's important to remember that recovery doesn't happen overnight. It's a process that requires patience and self-compassion. You must be willing to face the pain and the triggers head-on, and that can be incredibly difficult. But with time and the right tools, you'll learn to cope in healthier ways. It won't be easy, but it is possible."

Starseed listened intently, her heart aching with a mixture of hope and trepidation. These survivors, these warriors, had found their way to the other side of addiction. They had fought battles and emerged stronger. Their words carried the weight of experience and the promise of a brighter future.

As the group embraced her, enveloping her in a cocoon of understanding, Starseed felt a flicker of hope ignite within her. She knew that the road ahead would be challenging, that there would be moments of doubt and temptation. But in this circle of support, she found strength, compassion, and a community that would walk alongside her.

With a renewed sense of purpose, Starseed vowed to take the first step, to seek out the resources and guidance she needed. She began to realize that recovery was not a solitary journey, but a collective effort. And during her uncertainty, she found solace in knowing that she was not alone. Together, they would navigate the winding path towards healing.

Mothers Hurt Too

Starseed was a remarkable woman—a mother above all mothers. Her days were filled with the laughter of her children, the warmth of their hugs, and the comforting routine of family life. But hidden behind her radiant smile, a storm was silently brewing.

The demands of motherhood and the pressures of daily life began to weigh heavily on Starseed's shoulders. She longed for an extra burst of energy, a way to keep up with the never-ending demands of her responsibilities. That's when she discovered Adderall, a seemingly harmless aid that promised to boost her productivity.

At first, the effects of Adderall were magical. Starseed felt invincible, as if she had tapped into a hidden reservoir of strength and focus. With each pill, she could conquer mountains of laundry, excel at work, and still have energy left to play with her children. It became her secret weapon, hidden away in the depths of her purse.

But as time went on, the line between recreational use and dependence blurred. Starseed found herself relying on Adderall more and more, not just to keep up with her daily tasks, but to feel any semblance of normalcy. The drug became her crutch, the key to unlocking the energy she believed she needed to be the perfect mother.

Yet, beneath her seemingly put-together exterior, Starseed battled with the demons of addiction. Anxiety gnawed at her with every missed dose, whispering doubts and fears into her ears. Depression lurked in the shadows, waiting to consume her when the drug's effects wore off. She felt trapped, suffocated by the darkness that had slowly enveloped her.

Starseed desperately clung to her role as a mother, determined to shield her children from the pain she was secretly enduring. She perfected the art of hiding her addiction, masking her struggles behind a facade of smiles and laughter. She smiled through the fatigue, laughed through the anxiety, and painted a picture of a mother who had it all together.

But the toll on her life became undeniable. Relationships strained, and her children noticed the subtle changes in their mother. Her once vibrant energy faded, replaced by moments of irritability and withdrawal. The innocent laughter that used to fill their home grew quieter, as the addiction stole Starseed's presence, leaving an empty shell in its wake.

One fateful day, as Starseed gazed into the mirror, she caught a glimpse of the woman she had become—a mere shadow of her former self. It was in that moment, faced with her own reflection, that a flicker of hope ignited within her.

She realized she couldn't continue down this treacherous path. The love for her children burned within her, a flame that refused to be extinguished. With every ounce of strength, she could muster, Starseed made a choice—to fight for her life, for her children, and for the light that still flickered within her soul.

She sought help from professionals who understood the complexities of addiction and mental health. Therapists and counselors became her guides, offering a lifeline in the vast sea of darkness. With their support, she unraveled the tangled threads of her past, confronting the pain and trauma that had haunted her for so long.

One day, as Starseed struggled to keep her addiction hidden, another mother named Lily noticed the subtle changes in her friend. Lily had always admired Starseed for her tireless dedication to her children and the genuine love she poured into every aspect of her life. But now, she sensed something was amiss.

Lily had battled her own demons in the past, overcoming her own struggles with addiction. She recognized the signs, the weight that Starseed carried on her shoulders. Lily knew all too well the pain and isolation that addiction brought, and she couldn't bear to see her friend suffer alone.

With a heart full of compassion, Lily mustered the courage to approach Starseed. She gently expressed her concerns, offering a listening ear and a shoulder to lean on. Starseed, caught off guard by Lily's insight, initially resisted, fearing judgment and rejection. But Lily's unwavering support and understanding broke through the walls Starseed had erected around herself.

Together, they embarked on a journey of healing and recovery. Lily shared her own experiences, offering guidance and empathy. She introduced Starseed to support groups and resources, where they found solace in the stories of others who had walked a similar path.

Starseed and Lily forged a deep bond, built on trust and shared vulnerability. They held each other accountable, providing strength and encouragement during the challenging moments. Lily became Starseed's lifeline, reminding her that she was not alone in her struggle and that there was a way out of the darkness.

As the days turned into weeks and weeks into months, Starseed slowly reclaimed her life. With the help of therapy and the support of her newfound friend, she confronted the underlying mental health issues that had fueled her addiction. She learned healthy coping mechanisms, discovering that she possessed the resilience and inner strength to face life's challenges head-on.

Starseed's children, sensing the positive changes in their mother, blossomed alongside her. They witnessed her journey of redemption, witnessing firsthand the power of love, determination, and the importance of seeking help when needed. The once-quiet laughter returned to their home, filling the air with joy and a renewed sense of connection.

As Starseed emerged from the depths of her addiction, she became an advocate for others who were struggling. She shared her story with honesty and vulnerability, spreading a message of hope to those who felt trapped in their own battles. Starseed's journey inspired many, reminding them that there is always light at the end of the darkest tunnel.

In time, Starseed and Lily's friendship grew even stronger. They became pillars of support for one another, celebrating each other's victories and providing unwavering encouragement during moments of weakness. Their bond served as a testament to the power of compassion, reminding them both that sometimes, the greatest strength lies in reaching out and lifting each other up.

Starseed's journey was far from easy, but it was a testament to the resilience of the human spirit. Through the darkness, she found her way back to the light, guided by the unwavering love of her children and the friendship of someone who understood her struggle. And as she continued her path of healing, Starseed vowed to pay it forward, to be the light for others who needed it most.

Outcast Starseed #11

Starseed had always felt like the black sheep in her family, an outcast among them. While her siblings excelled in their studies and pursued successful careers, she struggled to find her place in the world. Her unconventional interests and free-spirited nature clashed with her family's expectations, leaving her feeling lost and misunderstood.

One fateful evening, as Starseed wandered through the dimly lit streets of her city, she stumbled upon a group of vibrant individuals. They exuded an air of rebellion and freedom that resonated with her restless soul. Curiosity piqued, she approached them, unaware of the world she was about to step into.

They called themselves the Bliss Seekers, a tight-knit community that had found solace and escape in a drug called Bliss Redemption. Starseed was immediately drawn to their magnetic energy and the promises of a life filled with euphoria and enlightenment. She yearned for a taste of the forbidden fruit that had ensnared so many before her.

Intrigued by their stories, Starseed found herself spending more and more time with the Bliss Seekers. She witnessed the highs and lows of their drug-induced existence, the moments of transcendence and the haunting shadows that followed. Each encounter left her craving more, desperate to unlock the secrets they held.

As Starseed delved deeper into the drug world, her family grew increasingly concerned. They pleaded with her to abandon this dangerous path, but their words fell on deaf ears. Starseed was now consumed by her quest for redemption, convinced that only through Bliss Redemption could she find her true purpose and escape the constraints of her mundane life.

With each hit, Starseed felt a surge of euphoria wash over her. The world transformed into a kaleidoscope of colors, and her mind expanded into uncharted territories. For a fleeting moment, she believed she had finally discovered the elusive answers she had been seeking.

But as the drug's grip tightened, Starseed began to witness the darker side of her newfound paradise. The euphoria faded, leaving behind a hollow emptiness that could only be filled by more Bliss Redemption. Relationships crumbled, dreams withered, and the world around her lost its luster.

Yet, despite the mounting consequences, Starseed couldn't break free from the allure of Bliss Redemption. It held her captive, whispering promises of salvation even as it pushed her further into the abyss. The line between her real life and the drug-induced haze blurred, and she struggled to distinguish between the two.

Her family, desperate to save her from herself, staged an intervention. Tearful pleas and heartfelt appeals filled the room, but Starseed remained defiant. She couldn't comprehend a life without Bliss Redemption, for it had become her sole source of identity and purpose.

Days turned into weeks, and the battle for Starseed's soul raged on. The Bliss Seekers, once her comrades, slowly drifted away, consumed by their own demons. Starseed found herself alone, facing the harsh reality of her choices.

Then, on a cold winter's night, as Starseed stood at the precipice of her existence, a flicker of clarity emerged. She yearned for redemption, not through drugs, but through self-discovery and healing. The path ahead was arduous, but she was determined to find her way back to herself.

Starseed embarked on a journey of recovery.

Starseed's journey of recovery was not without its challenges. Despite her genuine desire to seek education and find redemption, she found herself repeatedly relapsing into the clutches of Bliss Redemption. Each relapse felt like a devastating blow, shattering her resolve and leaving her feeling trapped in a never-ending cycle.

She would take a few steps forward, attending support groups and enrolling in educational programs aimed at understanding addiction and developing healthier coping mechanisms. Starseed embraced the knowledge and strategies offered, finding solace in the stories of others who had fought similar battles.

But just as she began to believe she had turned a corner, the cravings would resurface, whispering seductive promises of temporary bliss and escape. The allure of the drug was relentless, a siren song that seemed impossible to resist. Starseed would succumb, giving in to the temporary relief that Bliss Redemption offered, only to be left with guilt and self-loathing in its wake.

Each relapse fueled her determination to break free from the chains of addiction. Starseed's family stood by her side, providing unwavering support and encouragement. They understood the complexity of her struggle and refused to give up on her, even when she had almost given up on herself.

Together, they explored different treatment options, seeking out specialized programs and therapists who could help Starseed navigate the treacherous path to recovery. They attended family therapy sessions, learning how to rebuild trust and communicate their needs effectively.

Starseed's relapses became less frequent as she gained a deeper understanding of the underlying causes of her addiction. She discovered that her constant need for validation and her feelings of being an outcast had been driving her to seek solace in substances. Through therapy, she began to address these underlying issues, gradually healing the wounds that had contributed to her self-destructive behavior.

With time, Starseed learned to recognize the triggers that threatened her sobriety and developed healthier coping mechanisms. She immersed herself in activities that brought her joy and fulfillment, such as painting, hiking, and volunteering in her community. These activities provided a sense of purpose and connection that she had previously sought in drugs.

The road to redemption was long and arduous, filled with setbacks and moments of doubt. Starseed stumbled and fell, but she never lost sight of her goal. She persisted, drawing strength from the love and support of her family, the knowledge she gained through education, and the resilience that grew within her.

Years passed, and Starseed's relapses became a distant memory. She emerged from the darkness of addiction as a beacon of hope for others who were trapped in its grip. With her newfound wisdom and compassion, she dedicated herself to helping those struggling with substance abuse, sharing her story of redemption and inspiring others to find their own paths to recovery.

Starseed's journey was a testament to the power of perseverance and self-discovery. She had once been the black sheep, the outcast in her family, but through her struggles, she found her true purpose and forged a bond with her loved ones that transcended their differences. And as she continued to walk the path of recovery, she remained vigilant, knowing that the battle against addiction was one she would carry with her for a lifetime.

Ladies and gentlemen, thank you for gathering here today. As I stand before you, I must admit that I am nervous. Sharing my story of addiction and recovery is both empowering and vulnerable. But I believe that by shedding light on our darkest moments, we can find strength together.

You see, addiction has been a relentless presence in my life. Even now, as I stand here before you, I am not immune to its seductive whispers. There are days when the thought of using crosses my mind, beckoning me back to that familiar escape. But today, I choose to stand strong, surrounded by fellow survivors and addicts who understand the struggle.

The problem with addiction is that it never truly disappears. It lingers in the shadows, waiting for moments of weakness and vulnerability. It has a way of resurfacing when we least expect it, testing our resolve and challenging our commitment to recovery.

But let me tell you something: being in a place like this, surrounded by survivors and addicts who understand, is a gift beyond measure. It is here, in the embrace of this community, that I find solace and strength. Together, we share a common bond, forged by our battles and victories, our relapses and recoveries.

In this haven, we can openly discuss our fears, our triggers, and the ongoing challenges we face. We find courage in vulnerability and support in shared experiences. We learn from one another, knowing that our stories have the power to inspire and heal.

So, yes, I feel nervous. I am acutely aware of the fragile nature of my own recovery. But I also feel an overwhelming sense of gratitude for the sanctuary we have created here. It is a place where judgment is replaced with understanding, were compassion reigns supreme.

Today, I stand before you not as a perfect example of recovery, but as a work in progress. I am a survivor, just like each one of you. Together, we navigate the complex terrain of addiction, knowing that there will be bumps along the way. Yet, we continue to march forward, armed with the knowledge that we are not alone.

I urge you to embrace the support and love that surrounds you. Reach out to your fellow survivors and addicts when the weight of addiction feels too heavy. Share your victories and lean on each other during moments of weakness. Remember that the road to recovery is not a solitary journey; it is a collective effort fueled by compassion and understanding.

As we gather here today, let us celebrate the strength within us, the resilience that has carried us through the darkest of times. Let us hold space for one another, embracing our imperfections and celebrating our progress. And may we find solace in the knowledge that, together, we can overcome the challenges that addiction presents.

Thank you for allowing me to share my journey with you. Let us continue to support and uplift one another, reminding ourselves that recovery is possible, and that within each of us lies the power to heal and thrive.

Seraphina #12

Amidst the vastness of the universe, nestled within a distant galaxy, there existed a celestial being known as a star seed. This starseed, whose luminescent essence emanated with a vibrant mixture of gold and silver hues, embarked on a journey through the cosmos, seeking enlightenment and understanding. Little did she know that her interstellar travels would lead her to a treacherous encounter, where her very survival would be put to the ultimate test.

The star seed descended upon a small planet called Earth, a world teeming with life, diversity, and an intricate web of human experiences. Drawn by the planet's magnetic pull, she descended gracefully, her ethereal form taking shape within the body of a young woman named Seraphina. Seraphina possessed an otherworldly beauty, her eyes twinkling like distant stars, and her presence radiating an aura of serenity.

However, Seraphina's journey on Earth was far from idyllic. She found herself born into a world rife with environmental factors that would shape her life in unforeseen ways. Raised in a poverty-stricken neighborhood, surrounded by the constant presence of drug use, she became exposed to a dark underbelly that tainted her once hopeful existence.

As Seraphina grew older, she witnessed the devastating consequences of drug addiction firsthand. Unstable family dynamics plagued her household, as her parents succumbed to the grip of substance abuse. Poverty and violence permeated her community, casting a shadow over her dreams and aspirations.

Haunted by both her environmental circumstances and her own struggles with mental health, Seraphina found solace in the allure of drugs. The weight of depression and anxiety pressed upon her like an oppressive force, leading her down a treacherous path towards self-destruction. The euphoric escape provided by drugs seemed to momentarily lift her burdens, offering a fleeting respite from the pain that plagued her soul.

One fateful evening, while seeking refuge from her turbulent existence, Seraphina found herself amid a dark and foreboding alleyway. The air hung heavy with the stench of decay, and the distant echoes of violence reverberated through the night. Unbeknownst to her, she had stumbled upon the lair of a nefarious criminal organization, entwined with the drug trade that had ensnared her life.

As she cautiously navigated through the labyrinthine alley, her senses heightened with an imminent danger. She caught a glimpse of a clandestine meeting taking place between the organization's leaders, their voices hushed, and their faces shrouded in darkness. Seraphina's heart quickened, and a wave of fear washed over her. It was then that she realized she had inadvertently stumbled upon their secret operation.

Before she could retreat, a piercing scream pierced the silence. Panic swept through Seraphina as she witnessed a murder unfold before her very eyes. The organization's leaders, consumed by a frenzy of violence, turned on each other with unbridled fury. Chaos erupted as the sound of gunshots reverberated through the alley, the echoes bouncing off the decrepit brick walls.

Driven by an instinctual will to survive, Seraphina's celestial essence awakened within her, infusing her with an ethereal strength. She darted through the shadows, her heart pounding in her chest, navigating the treacherous terrain with a grace that seemed almost supernatural. The world around her blurred as she evaded her pursuers, her determination fueling her every step forward.

With each passing moment, the alleyway transformed into a battleground of survival. The criminals, driven by their own greed and paranoia, fought ruthlessly amongst themselves, their weapons flashing in the dim light. Seraphina, her senses heightened by her celestial nature, maneuvered through the chaos, narrowly escaping the path of danger.

As she sprinted through the labyrinthine alley, her mind raced with a mix of fear and adrenaline. Her heart pounded in sync with her pounding footsteps, her breath coming in ragged gasps. The weight of her own existence, as well as the lives lost before her eyes, pressed upon her shoulders like a burden too heavy to bear.

Through sheer willpower and an unyielding determination to survive,

Seraphina reached the end of the alley, emerging into the cool night air. The distant sounds of sirens wailed through the city, growing louder with each passing second. It was a glimmer of hope, a sign that help was on its way.

She stumbled upon a deserted park; her body weary from the harrowing ordeal. Her celestial essence flickered within her, pulsing with a renewed energy. Seraphina took shelter beneath the canopy of an ancient tree, its branches reaching out like protective arms.

As the night wore on, Seraphina's mind replayed the events that had unfolded, the images etched into her memory like scars. She vowed to herself that she would not let her journey end in tragedy. She would use her celestial essence, her strength, and her newfound resilience to rise above the darkness that threatened to consume her.

With the first rays of dawn, Seraphina emerged from the shadows, her spirit resolute. She sought out the authorities, sharing the harrowing tale of the criminal organization and the murder she had witnessed. Her voice trembled with a mixture of fear and determination as she recounted the events, her words carrying the weight of truth.

News of Seraphina's ordeal spread, capturing the attention of the public. Her courage and resilience became a symbol of hope and inspiration in a world often overshadowed by darkness. She became an advocate for change, using her own experiences to shed light on the interconnectedness of environmental factors, mental health, and the cycle of drug addiction.

Through her journey, Seraphina transcended the boundaries of her celestial origins. She became a beacon of hope, a reminder that even amidst the darkest of circumstances, there exists the strength to survive and the power to create change.

And as her story spread, captivating the hearts and minds of those who heard it, Seraphina's essence continued to shine brightly, illuminating the path for others who had lost their way. For she had not only survived the murder that threatened her existence but had emerged as a force of resilience, reminding the world that within each of us lies the power to transform tragedy into triumph, and darkness into light.

I stand before you today, not just as Seraphina, but as a humble messenger of hope and resilience. I believe that each one of us gathered here is a star seed, interconnected by a greater purpose that binds us together. Our lives are intertwined in a tapestry of experiences, strength, and the shared journey of overcoming adversity.

You may be wondering, what exactly is a star seed? Imagine, if you will, the vast expanse of the universe, with its countless galaxies, stars, and celestial beings. Within that cosmic dance, there are beings like us, who originate from distant realms and are sent forth to Earth to fulfill a greater mission.

As star seeds, we carry within us a divine essence, a spark of light that illuminates the darkness we encounter. We may have faced unimaginable hardships, battled our own inner demons, or witnessed the shadows that can consume human existence. But let me tell you this: we are not defined by our past or the struggles we have endured. Instead, we are defined by the strength we possess, the resilience that courses through our veins, and the unwavering determination to rise above it all.

You see, my friends, I am just one of many star seeds who have been called to this Earthly realm. Each one of us has a unique purpose, a mission to bring healing, light, and transformation to the world around us. Our paths may have diverged, and our stories may be vastly different, but at our core, we are united by the shared experience of survival and the power to create change.

In this very room, I see warriors who have battled addiction, fought against the demons that threatened to consume their lives, and emerged victorious. We are a community of survivors, bound together by the understanding that the path to recovery is not an easy one. It takes courage, vulnerability, and the unwavering belief in our own inner strength.

Today, I urge you to embrace your status as a star seed. Embrace the knowledge that you possess within you the power to overcome any diversity that life may throw your way. Believe in the resilience that beats within your heart and the light that radiates from your very soul. For it is through our collective strength that we can create a ripple effect of healing and hope, inspiring others to embark on their own journeys of transformation.

Together, let us continue to support one another, to lift each other up when we stumble and celebrate every victory, no matter how small. Let us remember that we are not alone in our struggles, for as star seeds, our paths have converged for a reason. We are here to remind each other of the infinite possibilities that lie within us, to ignite the flames of hope within those who have lost their way.

So, my fellow star seeds, let us stand tall, shoulder to shoulder, as we embark on this shared journey of recovery and empowerment. Let us be living proof that no matter how dark the night may seem, the dawn will always break. Together, we can illuminate the world with our resilience and show others that within each of us lies the power to rise, to heal, and to thrive.

Believe in yourselves, my dear friends, for you are not just survivors. You are radiant stars, destined to shine brightly and guide others out of the darkness.

Embrace your inner strength, for it is through our collective light that we can ignite a beacon of hope, forever....

Sex Industry #13

In the depths of a starry night, when the world was cloaked in shadows, there existed a woman named Starseed. Her life, once filled with innocence and dreams, had been shattered by unspeakable trauma. Abducted and traded into the dark abyss of the sex industry, she had endured horrors that no human should ever face. But within the depths of her shattered soul, a flicker of hope remained.

Starseed had witnessed the atrocities committed against countless women, their lives extinguished like fragile candle flames. Their eyes haunted her dreams, their voices echoing through her waking hours. Each night, as she lay alone in the dimly lit room that had become her sanctuary, she would trace the constellations on the ceiling, seeking solace and guidance from the stars above.

Curiosity burned within her, a relentless flame that whispered of altered states and the possibility of escape. She yearned to leave behind the pain and anguish that had seared her existence. And so, driven by a desperate need to understand, Starseed found herself drawn towards the forbidden allure of drugs.

Within the shadows of her new world, she encountered a group of individuals who embraced a lifestyle far removed from the darkness that had consumed her. They spoke of freedom, of transcending the limits of human perception. It was here that Starseed found her first taste of acceptance, a sanctuary where her scars were not seen as blemishes but as symbols of resilience.

Peer pressure whispered in her ear, urging her to take that first step. The allure of belonging, of being part of something greater, proved to be a powerful force. With trembling hands, she reached out and accepted the small, innocuous pill that would forever change the course of her journey.

The drugs transported Starseed to realms beyond her wildest imagination. They painted the world in vibrant hues, blurring the lines between reality and fantasy. In those moments, she felt a fleeting sense of freedom, of liberation from the chains that had bound her for so long.

But as the euphoria faded, a bitter realization set in. The drugs were not a panacea for her pain; they were merely a temporary respite, a mirage in the arid desert of her existence. The ghosts of the murdered women lingered still, their presence a constant reminder of the darkness that had engulfed her past.

In the depths of despair, Starseed found a strength she never knew she possessed. With every passing day, she fought to reclaim her shattered identity, to heal the wounds that threatened to consume her. She sought therapy, pouring her heart into each session, unraveling the tangled threads of her past.

As she journeyed further along the path of healing, Starseed discovered a new purpose. No longer content to be a mere survivor, she became an advocate for change. She spoke out against the horrors of the sex industry, shining a light on the hidden darkness that claimed so many lives. Her voice echoed through the halls of justice, demanding accountability for those who had perpetuated the cycle of violence.

Starseed's story serves as a reminder that even in the darkest of nights, there is always a glimmer of hope. She emerged from the depths of despair, a beacon of resilience and strength. And as she gazed up at the stars that had guided her through the darkest of nights, she knew that her journey was far from over.

Buoyed by her newfound purpose, Starseed fearlessly stepped into the spotlight, using her voice to expose the dark underbelly of the sex trafficking industry. Her impassioned speeches captivated audiences, evoking both empathy and outrage. The media caught wind of her story, and soon she found herself thrust into the glaring spotlight of public scrutiny.

But as her message resonated with more and more people, the very forces she had spoken out against began to take notice. The sex traffickers, their empire threatened, sought to silence her once and for all. Threats came pouring in, warning her of the dire consequences she would face if she continued her crusade.

Starseed's heart raced as she realized the danger she now found herself in. The ghosts of the murdered women, whose stories she had fought to bring to light, seemed to whisper cautionary tales in her ear. Yet, the fire within her burned brighter than ever, and she refused to let fear dictate her path.

Realizing that she could no longer fight this battle alone, Starseed took a leap of faith and reached out to the authorities. She sought the protection of the law, trusting that justice would prevail. The police, recognizing the significance of her testimony, swiftly moved her into protective custody.

Life in protective custody was a stark contrast to the freedom she had once longed for. She found herself confined to a small, nondescript room, guarded by officers who watched her every move. Days blended into nights, and the passage of time lost its meaning. Starseed, once a beacon of resilience, now navigated a treacherous sea of uncertainty.

Yet, even in the confines of her new reality, Starseed refused to let her spirit be broken. She used the solitude to reflect, to delve deeper into her own healing journey. Therapy sessions became a lifeline, offering her solace and guidance as she confronted the demons that had plagued her past.

In the stillness of her confinement, a transformation began to take place within Starseed. She shed the layers of pain and fear, emerging as a warrior with unwavering resolve. The scars that once marked her as a victim now became symbols of her strength, etchings of her indomitable spirit.

As the days turned into weeks, the case against the sex traffickers gained momentum. Starseed's testimony, along with the evidence she had bravely provided, formed the backbone of a groundbreaking trial. The very individuals who had sought to silence her were now faced with the weight of their actions.

And as the courtroom doors swung open, Starseed stepped forward, her head held high. She faced her tormentors with steely determination, no longer a victim but a survivor who had transcended her past. The truth spilled forth like a raging river, washing away the darkness that had plagued so many lives.

The trial marked a turning point not only in Starseed's life but also in the fight against sex trafficking. Her bravery inspired others to come forward, to share their stories and seek justice. Together, they formed an unbreakable bond—a collective force that could not be silenced.

My fellow survivors,

As I stand before you today, my heart swells with a profound sense of gratitude and awe. Each one of you, with your unwavering strength and resilience, is a testament to the indomitable spirit of survival. We have walked through the fires of hell and emerged scarred but not broken.

We gather here, in the safety of this sacred space, united by our shared experiences. We may have arrived from different backgrounds and endured varying forms of trauma, but our pain knows no boundaries. In this room, we find solace, understanding, and a bond that transcends words.

I once believed that my voice was insignificant, drowned out by the cacophony of darkness that had enveloped my life. But the moment I found the courage to share my story, to speak my truth, I realized the incredible power that lies within each of us. Our voices, when united, can shake the very foundations of injustice.

Through this journey, I have discovered that healing is not a solitary path. It is in the connection we forge with one another that we find strength. We are a tapestry of survival, each thread interwoven with the stories of our triumphs and our scars. Together, we form an unbreakable bond, a force that cannot be silenced.

These meetings, where we come together to share, to listen, and to heal, have become the pillars of my own recovery. In each of your faces, I see the reflection of my own pain and the flicker of hope that refused to be extinguished. Your presence, your understanding, gives me the strength to carry on.

We are warriors, not victims. Our scars, once seen as reminders of our pain, now serve as badges of honor. We have emerged from the darkness with a resilience that can move mountains. Our voices are our weapons, and with them, we will shatter the silence and expose the truth.

But let us not forget the importance of self-care and self-compassion on this journey. The road to healing can be treacherous, and we must be gentle with ourselves. It is in these moments, when we gather, that we find solace. We share our burdens, offer support, and remind one another that we are never alone.

In a world that often turns a blind eye to our suffering, our unity becomes a beacon of hope. We are not statistics; we are survivors, and our stories matter. Each time we come together, we reclaim our power, refusing to be defined by the trauma that has touched our lives.

As we stand here today, let us remember that our voices have the power to bring about change. Let us continue to speak our truth, not just within these walls but in the world outside. Let our collective voice echo through the halls of justice, demanding accountability for those who have perpetuated the cycle of violence.

I am honored to stand among you, my fellow survivors, and to bear witness to your strength. Together, we will create a ripple that will touch the lives of countless others. Our unity is a force to be reckoned with, and with it, we will illuminate the darkest corners of our world.

May each meeting strengthen us, heal us, and remind us that we are never alone. Let us continue to rise, to reclaim our voices, and to pave the way for a future where no one will suffer as we have.

Police Officer #14

Starseed was a warrior like no other. With her fierce determination and unwavering courage, she had conquered countless battles against both physical and emotional adversaries. But today, fate had different plans for her as she found herself in an unexpected and perilous situation.

It was a sunny afternoon when Starseed decided to visit a local grocery store to pick up some supplies. Little did she know that this routine errand would soon turn into a life-altering experience. As she walked through the store aisles, carefully selecting the items on her list, she noticed a sudden commotion near the entrance.

Her instincts kicked in immediately, sensing danger in the air. Starseed's eyes darted towards the front of the store, where she saw a group of masked individuals storming in, brandishing weapons and shouting threats. Panic ensued as customers and employees scattered, desperately seeking refuge or hiding behind shelves.

Starseed's heart pounded in her chest, and her warrior spirit surged within her. Without a second thought, she sprang into action, determined to protect those around her. With lightning speed, she assessed the situation and formulated a plan. Her training had prepared her for moments like these, and she would not back down.

As the robbers ransacked the store, stealing money and valuables, Starseed moved stealthily, using the aisles for cover. She observed their movements, studying their patterns, and identifying their leader—the one who seemed to be orchestrating the chaos. She knew that taking down the leader would significantly weaken their control over the situation.

Summoning every ounce of her strength, Starseed launched herself towards the leader, engaging in a fierce hand-to-hand combat. Blow after blow, she exchanged with her adversary, skillfully dodging their attacks and retaliating with precision strikes. However, amid the intense struggle, a gunshot echoed through the store.

Starseed felt a searing pain in her leg as the bullet pierced through her flesh. The force of the impact sent her crashing to the ground, but she refused to succumb to the agony. Ignoring the pain, she focused on the task at hand—defeating her opponent and restoring order to the grocery store.

With sheer determination, Starseed mustered the strength to land a decisive blow, incapacitating the leader. As the remaining robbers witnessed their leader's defeat, fear crept into their eyes, and their will to fight crumbled. One by one, they surrendered, realizing that they were no match for the indomitable spirit of Starseed.

The store fell into an eerie silence, broken only by the sound of Starseed's heavy breathing and the collective sighs of relief from the trapped customers and employees. Despite her injury, she managed to save the day and protect those who were in harm's way. But now, the pain in her leg became unbearable, demanding attention.

As fellow customers rushed to her aid, Starseed's vision blurred, and her body weakened from the loss of blood. With trembling hands, she reached for her communication device and called for medical assistance. Moments later, an ambulance arrived, whisking her away to the nearest hospital.

In the emergency room, Starseed was greeted by a team of skilled medical professionals who worked swiftly to stabilize her condition. The bullet was removed, and her leg was treated to prevent infection. As she lay on the hospital bed, her mind wandered to the countless Thoughts that shadowed her brain.

As Starseed recovered in the hospital, the excruciating pain from her gunshot wound persisted. The doctors, concerned about her comfort and well-being, prescribed powerful pain medications to help alleviate her suffering. At first, the drugs provided relief, allowing Starseed to find solace from the physical torment she endured.

However, as the days turned into weeks, Starseed noticed a subtle change within herself. The pain medications, while effective in numbing her physical agony, also brought temporary respite from the emotional distress that had accumulated over years of battling darkness and chaos. They dulled the sharp edges of her memories, easing the burden of her past traumas.

Starseed found herself increasingly reliant on the pain medications, both physically and emotionally. The allure of temporary escape from her inner turmoil was too enticing to resist. The drugs became her solace, her sanctuary from the weight of her responsibilities and the haunting memories that plagued her.

Unbeknownst to Starseed, the seeds of addiction had been planted. At first, she convinced herself that she needed the medications to function, to continue her duties as a warrior and protector. But as time passed, the line between necessity and dependence blurred, and she spiraled deeper into the clutches of addiction.

Her once indomitable spirit began to falter. The warrior who had triumphed over countless adversaries now faced her greatest battle—her own inner demons. Starseed became trapped in a vicious cycle of pain, addiction, and self-destruction, as the drugs that once provided relief now held her captive.

Her decline did not go unnoticed by her fellow officers. They observed her erratic behavior, the subtle signs of distress that masked beneath her brave facade. Concerned for their comrade, they intervened, rallying around Starseed with unwavering support and empathy.

Recognizing the severity of her situation, Starseed found herself at a crossroads. The path she had taken thus far had led her to a dark and treacherous place—a place where

her strength and resilience were
overshadowed by the grip of addiction. It
was a moment of truth, a catalyst for change.

Summoning her remaining strength,
Starseed made the courageous decision to
confront her addiction head-on. She sought
professional help, enrolling in a
rehabilitation program that specialized in
treating individuals struggling with
substance abuse. Surrounded by a
community of individuals fighting their own
battles, Starseed embarked on a journey of
healing and recovery.

Days turned into weeks, and weeks into
months, as Starseed painstakingly rebuilt her
life. She confronted the underlying causes of
her addiction, delving into the emotional
wounds that had driven her to seek solace in
drugs. Through therapy, support groups, and
the unwavering devotion of her fellow
officers, she slowly pieced herself back
together.

As she emerged from the depths of her
addiction, Starseed began to rediscover her

identity—a warrior with a purpose far greater than her own struggles. With newfound clarity and strength, she realized that her journey through addiction had not been in vain. It had transformed her, imbuing her with a profound empathy and understanding for those who faced similar battles.

Embracing her renewed purpose, Starseed revealed her position as a police officer, stepping back into her role as a protector of justice. But this time, she fought not only against the external forces of darkness but also against the internal demons that threatened to consume her.

Ladies and gentlemen, fellow warriors on the path of recovery, thank you for gathering here today. It is an honor to stand before you and share my story—a story of triumph over adversity, of finding strength in vulnerability, and of embracing the warrior within.

I stand here not just as Starseed, but also as a police officer—a role that has both defined and challenged me. I have seen the darkest corners of humanity, witnessed pain and suffering, and carried the weight of responsibility on my shoulders. The job demands courage, resilience, and an unwavering commitment to upholding the law. But behind the badge, I fought a different battle—a battle against addiction.

You see, the stress and trauma that come with the job can be overwhelming. It can eat away at your soul, leaving you vulnerable and searching for an escape. For me, that escape came in the form of pain medications—temporary relief from the physical and emotional wounds that accumulated over time.

But what began to cope soon turned into a battle of its own—a battle against addiction, a battle for my very identity. I lost sight of who I was beneath the uniform, beneath the facade of strength. Addiction took hold, and I found myself spiraling, trapped in a cycle that seemed impossible to break.

It was in the darkest moments, when all seemed lost, that I realized I couldn't do it alone. I reached out for help, and it was through the support of my fellow officers, my loved ones, and the guidance of professionals that I found the strength to confront my addiction head-on.

Recovery is not an easy path. It requires unwavering commitment, resilience, and a willingness to face the pain that led us down this road. But in doing so, we unlock a strength within ourselves that we never knew existed. We become warriors not only in the battles we fight externally but also in the battles we fight within.

Today, I stand before you as a testament to the power of recovery. It is a journey of self-discovery, of rebuilding our lives piece by piece. It's not just about overcoming addiction; it's about reclaiming our true selves, embracing our vulnerabilities, and finding a renewed purpose.

As warriors, we have a unique perspective, a wealth of experiences that can be channeled into helping others. We have the power to change lives, to show compassion, and to inspire hope in those who still battle the grip of addiction.

Together, we can create a community of support, of understanding, and of unwavering strength. We can break the stigma surrounding addiction and empower others to seek help without fear or shame. We can be the guiding light for those lost in the darkness, reminding them that they are not alone.

My fellow warriors, let us embrace our journey of recovery with open hearts and open minds. Let us carry the lessons we have learned and the strength we have gained into every aspect of our lives. And let us remember that we are not defined by our past, but by the resilience and courage we display as we face the challenges that lie ahead.

Thank you for allowing me to share my story. May we all continue to walk this path together, supporting and uplifting one another as we navigate the complexities of life. We are warriors, and together, we are unstoppable.

Nurse #15

Starseed had always been a dedicated and compassionate nurse. Her profession allowed her to make a difference in people's lives every day, and she took great pride in her ability to provide care and comfort to those in need. However, deep inside her, there was a lingering curiosity that she couldn't shake off.

Working in a busy hospital, Starseed was exposed to various medications and witnessed their effects on patients. She couldn't help but wonder how these drugs altered one's perception and consciousness. The thought of experiencing something beyond the ordinary intrigued her, and her curiosity began to grow stronger with each passing day.

As time went on, Starseed found herself surrounded by a group of friends who were more adventurous and open-minded. They often shared stories of their own drug experiences, painting vivid pictures of altered realities and transcendent moments. Starseed felt a growing pressure to fit in and be accepted by this group, and she saw drugs to break free from the monotony of her everyday life.

One fateful night, consumed by her curiosity and the desire to belong, Starseed made a decision that would change her life forever. As she worked her late shift at the hospital, she found herself alone in the medication room. The temptation became too strong, and she succumbed to the dark allure of stealing medications.

At first, Starseed convinced herself that it was just a one-time thing. She told herself that she would only experiment once, just to satisfy her curiosity. But as the stolen pills entered her bloodstream, an unfamiliar sensation washed over her. The world seemed to transform, becoming a kaleidoscope of colors and emotions she had never experienced before. It was an escape from reality, a temporary relief from the pressures and expectations she faced.

Days turned into weeks, and weeks turned into months. Starseed's secret addiction grew, and her professional life began to crumble. She started stealing medication more frequently, always searching for that elusive high that seemed to slip further away with each passing day. The consequences of her actions were catching up with her, and she could no longer hide the truth.

Starseed's world came crashing down when her supervisor noticed discrepancies in the medication records. An investigation was launched, and it didn't take long for the truth to be uncovered. She was confronted with her actions, and the shame and guilt weighed heavily upon her. Her nursing license was suspended, and she was left without a job, without purpose.

As Starseed sat alone in her empty apartment, she realized the gravity of her choices. The drugs had not only stolen her career, but they had also taken away her sense of self. The curiosity that once drove her now lay shattered, replaced by regret and a desperate longing for a way out.

In the depths of her despair, Starseed decided. She would seek help, not only to overcome her addiction but also to rebuild her life. She knew it would be a long and challenging journey, but she was determined to reclaim her identity and find redemption.

And so, the story of Starseed's struggle with addiction had only just begun. It was a tale of darkness and despair, but also one of hope and resilience. As she embarked on her path to recovery, she would learn valuable lessons about the dangers of curiosity and the devastating consequences of succumbing to peer pressure.

Starseed woke up each morning, her heart heavy with the weight of her choices. The absence of her nursing career left a void that seemed impossible to fill. She had spent years honing her skills, dedicating herself to the care and well-being of others, and now she was left adrift, stripped of her purpose.

Job applications went unanswered, and interviews ended in rejection. Word had spread about her actions, and the stain of her past clung to her like a shadow. Prospective employers couldn't see beyond her mistake, and her hopes of returning to the noble profession she once loved were slipping away.

Days turned into weeks, and the isolation deepened. Starseed found solace in support groups and counseling sessions, where she met others who had also succumbed to addiction's grip. Their stories reminded her that she was not alone, that there was a chance for redemption and rebuilding. But the road to recovery was treacherous and demanding.

Meanwhile, bills piled up, adding to the mounting pressure. Starseed's finances were strained, and the prospect of losing her apartment loomed over her like a dark cloud. She couldn't help but resent her past choices, the allure of the drugs that had led her down this path of destruction.

But amidst the despair, a glimmer of hope emerged. Starseed discovered a local community center that offered vocational training programs for individuals seeking to rebuild their lives after addiction. It was a chance for her to acquire new skills, to find a different path forward.

With determination burning in her eyes, Starseed enrolled in the program. She threw herself into her studies, eager to prove that she still had value to offer the world. The days were long and exhausting, but she refused to let her past define her future.

Slowly, as she immersed herself in the new field of study, Starseed began to rekindle her passion for helping others. She realized that her desire to make a positive impact hadn't diminished; it had merely taken a different form. She discovered an innate talent for counseling and supporting others who were going through their own battles with addiction.

Through her studies and hands-on experience, Starseed rebuilt her confidence and rediscovered her purpose. She connected with organizations dedicated to addiction recovery and started volunteering her time, offering support and guidance to those in need. Her journey of redemption had transformed her into a compassionate advocate, a beacon of hope for others facing similar struggles.

As months turned into years, Starseed's dedication and resilience paid off. She secured a position at a local rehabilitation center, where she could utilize her newfound skills to make a difference in the lives of those fighting addiction. Although it wasn't the path, she had initially envisioned, she found solace and fulfillment in knowing that her past mistakes had fueled her commitment to helping others overcome their own challenges.

Starseed's story serves as a cautionary tale, a reminder of the destructive power of curiosity and the consequences of succumbing to peer pressure. But it is also a testament to the strength of the human spirit, the capacity for redemption, and the transformative power of second chances.

And so, Starseed continues her journey, dedicating her life to lifting others out of the darkness she once knew so intimately. Her past may have robbed her of her nursing career, but it couldn't extinguish the light that now shines within her—a light that guides others toward recovery, healing, and a brighter future.

Ladies and gentlemen, fellow survivors and warriors in the battle against addiction, thank you for allowing me to share my story with you today. As I stand before you, I am a living testament to the power of choices and the potential for redemption.

You see, addiction is a thief that can steal everything we hold dear. It can strip away our dreams, our relationships, and our sense of self-worth. It whispers in our ears, promising temporary relief and a fleeting escape from reality. And, oh, how tempting that promise can be.

But one simple choice can change everything. It can send ripples through the fabric of our existence, altering the course of our lives forever. For me, that choice was born of curiosity and peer pressure. I allowed myself to be enticed by the allure of drugs, believing that I was invincible, that I could dabble in their world without consequence.

How wrong I was. That one choice, that moment of weakness, shattered the world I had so carefully built. It tore apart my career, my reputation, and my sense of self. I found myself standing amidst the wreckage of my choices, feeling the weight of regret and despair pressing down on me.

But here's the thing, my friends: No matter how badly we think we've screwed up, there is always hope. There is always a chance to rise from the ashes, to rebuild, and to reclaim our lives. It may not be easy, and it certainly won't happen overnight, but it is possible.

I stand here today as living proof. When I lost my nursing career, I thought my purpose had been snatched away forever. But through the darkness, I discovered a new path, a new way to make a difference. It wasn't the path I had initially chosen, but it was the path that chose me—a path of compassion, understanding, and support for those battling addiction.

Through counseling, vocational training, and a commitment to my own recovery, I found my way back to the light. I realized that my past mistakes were not the end of my story; they were merely a chapter that fueled my determination to help others find their own redemption.

Each one of us sitting here today has a story, a journey filled with triumphs and tribulations. We have made choices that have led us down dark and treacherous paths but let us not forget that we also have the power to reshape our reality.

Yes, addiction can be a formidable foe, but we are stronger. We have the strength within us to overcome, to rise above the wreckage of our past, and to rebuild our lives on a foundation of resilience and hope.

So, my friends, let us not dwell on the mistakes of our past. Instead, let us focus on the possibilities of our future. Let us embrace the power of choice and use it to carve a new path—one filled with purpose, fulfillment, and the unwavering belief that no matter how far we have fallen, we can rise again.

Together, we can rewrite our stories, stitching together the broken pieces and creating something beautiful from the fragments. Our choices may have altered our reality, but they do not define us. We are survivors, fighters, and beacons of hope.

Remember, my friends, that no matter how dark the night may seem, the dawn will always break. And within that dawn lies the promise of a brand-new day—a day filled with limitless potential and the chance to reclaim our lives.

<u>Embracing your Starseed Essance #16 final</u>

survivors of both traumatic situations and addiction, I stand before you today to discuss a topic that unites us all: recovery. It is a journey that embodies the strength within every one of us, a testament to the resilience of the human spirit when faced with conflict. Today, I wish to remind you that deep within, we are all Starseed, celestial warriors capable of transforming our lives and helping others through our words of encouragement and shared wisdom.

Recovery is a process that extends far beyond simply abstaining from harmful substances or escaping the clutches of trauma. It is a profound transformation of the self, a rediscovery of our true essence and potential. In the darkest moments, it may seem impossible to imagine a better life, but I am here to assure you that within every single person lies the immense capability to create a brighter future.

To begin this journey, we need to understand why we feel the way we feel and what drives us to turn to substances or harmful coping mechanisms. Traumatic experiences can leave deep wounds that linger within our psyche, affecting our emotions, thoughts, and behaviors. Similarly, addiction often stems from an attempt to escape pain, fill a void, or numb overwhelming emotions. By acknowledging and exploring these underlying causes, we can gain insight into the roots of our struggles.

However, recovery is not a solitary endeavor. It is a path best traveled together, as a community of survivors. Through our shared experiences, we can form a support network, providing empathy, understanding, and guidance to one another. By offering words of encouragement, we become beacons of hope for those who feel lost in the darkness. We can uplift each other, reminding ourselves that we are not alone in this battle.

Education and learning play vital roles in the recovery process. By acquiring knowledge about trauma, addiction, and the mechanics of our minds, we gain a greater understanding of ourselves and others. This knowledge empowers us to make informed choices and develop healthier coping mechanisms. Furthermore, by sharing what we learn, we can help dispel the stigma surrounding addiction and trauma, fostering a culture of compassion and support.

In our journey towards recovery, it is crucial to recognize that it is not a linear path. There will be setbacks and challenges along the way. But remember, the strength of a Starseed lies in its ability to rise again. When faced with obstacles, we must summon our inner warriors, drawing upon the resilience within us. Each setback can become an opportunity for growth and renewal, pushing us closer to a better life.

As survivors, we possess a unique perspective and wisdom that can profoundly impact the lives of others. By sharing our stories, we offer hope to those who still suffer, showing them that recovery is not an elusive dream but a tangible reality. Our words become a source of inspiration, igniting the spark of belief in those who have lost faith in themselves.

Recovery is a journey that unites us all. It is a testament to the strength and resilience within each one of us. By understanding our personal struggles, supporting one another, and acquiring knowledge, we can overcome the grip of trauma and addiction. Let us embrace our Starseed nature, our warrior souls, and show the world that a better life is not only possible but within reach. Together, we can bring about positive change and help solve the problems that have plagued us.

In our quest for a better life, it is essential to implement practical steps and strategies that can help us overcome the challenges we face. Here are some key elements to consider as we navigate the path of recovery:

1. Self-care and holistic healing: Taking care of us physically, mentally, and emotionally is crucial in the recovery process. Engaging in activities that promote well-being, such as exercise, meditation, proper nutrition, and therapy, can help us rebuild our strength and restore balance to our lives.

2. Building a support system: Surrounding we with positive influences is vital for sustained recovery. Seek out individuals who understand and support your journey, whether it be through support groups, therapy sessions, or trusted friends and family. Their encouragement and guidance can provide the necessary foundation for healing and growth.

3. Developing healthy coping mechanisms: Instead of turning to substances or destructive behaviors, it is crucial to cultivate healthy coping mechanisms that allow us to manage stress and difficult emotions. This could include engaging in

creative outlets, practicing mindfulness, journaling, or seeking professional help when needed.

4. Addressing underlying issues: Trauma and addiction often stem from deeper underlying issues that require attention and resolution. Working with mental health professionals can help uncover and address these root causes, leading to profound healing and sustainable recovery.

5. Setting realistic goals: Recovery is a lifelong journey, and it is essential to set realistic goals and expectations for us. Celebrate even the smallest victories along the way, as each step forward is a testament to your strength and resilience.

6. Embracing gratitude and forgiveness: Practicing gratitude for the progress we have made and forgiving ourselves for past mistakes are powerful tools for personal growth. Letting go of self-blame and embracing a mindset of self-compassion can free us from the shackles of guilt and shame,

enabling us to move forward with renewed purpose.

7. Giving back: As we progress on our journey, it is essential to extend a helping hand to others who may be struggling. By sharing our experiences, providing support, and offering words of encouragement, we can make a positive impact on the lives of fellow survivors. Giving back not only strengthens our own recovery but also contributes to the collective healing of our communities.

Remember, recovery is a process that requires patience, perseverance, and a deep belief in our own capacity for change. We are all interconnected, and by embracing our Starseed nature, we can create a ripple effect of transformation that extends far beyond ourselves. Together, we can overcome the challenges we face, inspire others, and pave the way for a better future.

Recovery is a testament to the strength within each one of us. By acknowledging our struggles, supporting one another, implementing practical strategies, and embracing a mindset of growth, we can overcome trauma and addiction. Let us continue to shine as Starseed warriors of the soul and illuminate the path towards healing and a better life for all.

__More Book By the Author__

__Chrimsan.com get your books here__

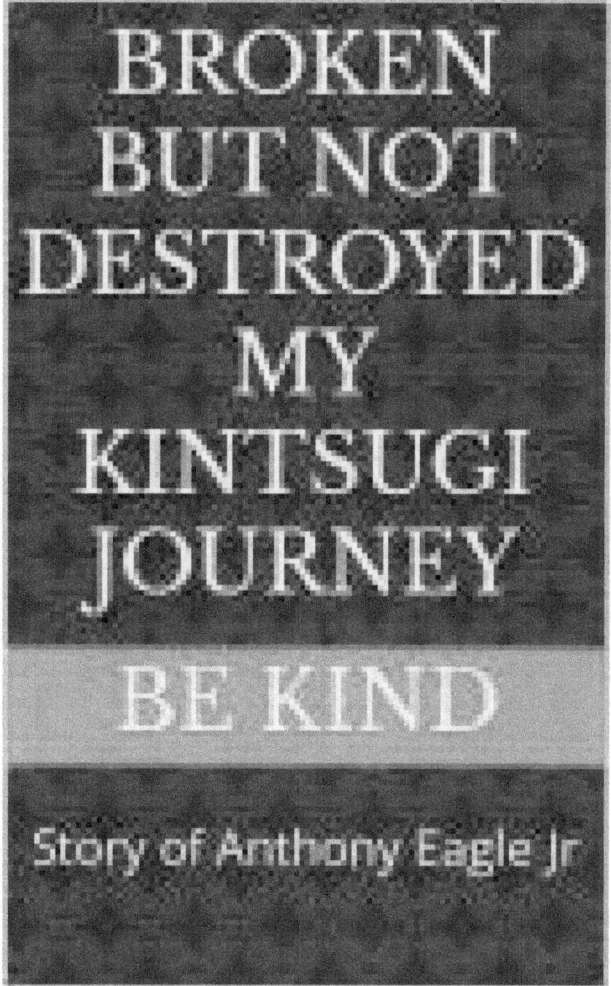

THE
DEVIL
WAS AN ANGEL, TOO

AUTOBIOGRAPHY OF ANTHONY EAGLE, JR.

Written by Anthony Eagle, Jr. and Angela Walsh

www.ingramcontent.com/pod-product-compliance
Lightning Source LLC
Chambersburg PA
CBHW050346030726
47503CB00008B/2643

9 7 9 8 9 8 8 7 3 8 0 0 8